WHITE COLLAR RANCHER

PART-TIME COWBOYS, BOOK 3

MARIE JOHNSTON

LE PUBLISHING

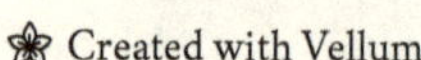 Created with Vellum

Friends with benefits never hurt anyone, right?

Justin used to rule the boardroom. Now he rules his own little plot of land, or he could if he weren't a clueless single dad with a newborn. Desperate for help, he calls out an SOS to an old friend—the doctor who delivered his son. But the longer she's around, the harder it is to ignore that a stunning intellect isn't her only appeal.

It was supposed to be just two friends getting through a baby's colic together. Only Priya has harbored way more than friendly feelings for Justin for years, and she's struggling to keep her thoughts platonic around the scruffy, rugged rancher. It doesn't hurt that he's the only friendly port in a frigid small town that was supposed to welcome her back with open arms.

Justin's sworn off women and refuses to change for anyone. Priya's fighting to save her job and has no time to soothe male egos. So a friends-with-benefits arrangement seems like the perfect solution…except no one warned them one of the "benefits" could be a broken heart.

CHAPTER 1

"*J*ustin, you need to get to the emergency room."

Priya's direct tone cut through his quiet night streaming the fourth season of *Longmire*. She was using her doctor's tone. He teased her about it during each prenatal visit. Priya was Maisy's doctor and that helped take the sting out of each grueling appointment with the unstable, untrustworthy mom of his kid.

But the ER? Justin's heart clawed into his throat. If Maisy was going into labor, she was supposed to be admitted to the maternity wing, not the ER.

"What's wrong?" He was already off the couch, stuffing his feet into his dusty cowboy boots. Forgoing a jacket, he banged out the front door. The house would have to stay unlocked. He lived too far out of town for trespassers to be a problem, but it was habit from living in Denver. Besides, his neighbors were all cousins and the land that bordered the back of his own property was his brother's.

Priya's curt words spurred him into a jog. "Maisy's sick and we're taking the baby. I don't… I don't know if she's going to make it." The hitch nearly stopped him short. Priya was talking about Maisy, her friend since high school, and trying to hold it together. The three of them had hung out together back then, but nowadays, they were only together during Maisy's OB visits. His ex was a scourge in his life, but he didn't want harm to come to her, whether she was carrying his child or not.

"What's going on, Priya?"

"I've got to go. Someone will explain when you arrive, but get here now." The line went dead.

Hard reality sank in as he fired up his pickup and stomped on the gas.

Maisy was so sick they were delivering his son.

The trip was a blur. He had no idea what was going on and his mind conjured the worst, only he didn't know what the worst was. His baby wasn't supposed to come for two weeks. Maisy had refused to settle on a name—another controlling tactic of hers. Her moods had been erratic throughout the pregnancy, swinging from saccharine sweet and apologetic for her outbursts to enraged and jealous that he refused to propose to her—or to even label her his girl-friend. Because she wasn't.

She had been, then he'd discovered what a two-faced, mean-spirited woman she was and look at that. Now she was pregnant despite his religious use of condoms.

One weak moment when he'd turned to her after—

Well, thinking about his ex in Denver, who was living the good life with the other half of the company they'd built together, wasn't going to help.

He'd made it through the last thirty-eight weeks telling himself that he'd endure Maisy for the baby. But shifting from endurance to concern for the woman sent his mind spinning. Priya hadn't said an accident, or early labor, but sick. What was she sick with? She'd been perfectly healthy three days ago at her last prenatal visit.

He swung into the hospital. The lot was sprinkled with cars, but the idea that he wasn't the only one whose life was changing course tonight didn't make him feel better.

He rushed inside, slipping through the sliding door the moment there was enough of a gap for him. His boots echoed through the quiet entry. Squinting against the shine of the fluorescent lights, he ignored the three other people in the waiting room. They were scattered among the thirty empty chairs, hunched over or slouched in their seats. He probably knew them, since he'd grown up in Moore, Minnesota, population just under five digits.

A young guy in maroon scrubs watched his approach from behind a wide desk with a plexiglass panel that reached to the ceiling. Justin went straight for the opening.

"Justin Walker." He said it like his name was a password. Would he get in? He wasn't Maisy's significant anything, but surely baby daddy was enough.

The guy nodded. "Right. Dr. Patel's expecting you, but she wants you to head to the surgical waiting room."

The guy gave him directions, but all that registered was where he pointed. Justin spun on his heel and strode away. He'd been born in this hospital; surely he could find the way.

Two wrong turns later, he rounded a corner. The area was smaller than the ER waiting room. A coffee machine sat empty and the TV was off.

The sight flooded his system with dread. During one of Maisy's appointments, Priya had explained that she could perform a C-section, even an emergency C-section, in Moore's one and only hospital, but he'd never thought it would happen.

Maisy's parents were tucked into a corner of the sparse waiting room. Their pale faces and red-rimmed eyes told him the news was not good.

Justin didn't bother with formalities. Her parents weren't

his biggest fans and he had no idea what story Maisy was telling them. Was he a good guy or a bad guy to them? "What's going on?"

Katherine Jorgenson sucked in a shaky breath and clutched her husband's hand. "They, uh…they said she has meningitis and she's not…she won't…" Her head bowed, and sobs shook her shoulders.

Martin Jorgenson took over. There was no inflection in his tone. "She waited too long to come in, they said. They were losing her in the ER, but, um—" His face crumpled. "They're saving the baby."

Justin crouched in front of them. He stared at the floor. They'd been losing her in the ER when Priya had called. Understanding wasn't coming easy. Maisy was Maisy. She was indomitable. He'd pondered her sanity several times over the last nine months, but she was too full of life to die.

He knew next to nothing about meningitis. Wasn't it an infection in the spine or something? And deadly. He knew that much.

Katherine sniffled. "She complained about an ear infection, but she didn't want to take meds. Afraid of hurting the baby. Wouldn't listen—" She broke down again.

"The doctor said that this type of meningitis can start that way," Martin filled in. "And it can move fast. And Maisy's so stubborn."

Justin bobbed his head and rose enough to sit adjacent to them. "The baby?"

"Isaiah's heartbeat was strong," Katherine replied. "Priya thinks he has a good chance."

"Isaiah?"

Katherine shot him a confused glance as tears coursed down her cheeks. "Isaiah. Your son."

"I… I didn't realize she'd chosen a name."

"Isaiah Martin Jorgenson." Katherine cleared her throat.

"Of course she mentioned putting Walker on the birth certificate if you decided to propose."

That was never going to happen.

His world darkened and guilt flooded in. That was never going to happen if she was dead. Maisy couldn't die. She was the mother of his child. He hadn't planned for one second to leave her to raise their kid by herself. Never would he have thought that *he'd* be alone.

She couldn't leave him to raise a kid by himself. What did he know about babies? What did he know about raising a son whose mom had died giving birth to him? He'd been prepared for talks about why Daddy and Mommy weren't together, maybe defending his right to co-parent if she tried to play her games with… Isaiah.

He tested out the name.

His heart pounded. This wasn't his life. He'd moved back to Moore to slow down. Less world travel. Less drama after he'd fallen stupidly in love only to get his company stolen, his heart ripped out, and his body driven into Maisy's waiting embrace. The move home was supposed to have stabilized his life, not upended it.

The door into the surgery unit opened. Priya's normally warm brown eyes were destroyed. Her expression was stoic, but she vibrated with restrained emotion. The woman in front of him wanted so badly to break down, but she knew she couldn't yet. She wore the same maroon scrubs as the guy downstairs, and her rich black hair was bundled into a bun on top of her head. Her thick, dark lashes only shadowed the depth of grief in her eyes.

The scrubs bothered him. Priya wasn't a casual woman. She'd hadn't been that way when they were kids, and during Maisy's office visits, Priya always wore professional clothing underneath her pristine white lab coat.

Scrubs and athletic shoes. Funny how they cemented how serious this situation was.

Maisy was Priya's best friend, though the last year and Maisy's mental state had tested the bond. They weren't close like they used to be. He'd gotten the impression that, like him, Priya was only committed to Maisy's well-being during pregnancy and the baby's health.

She met his gaze. Hers wavered like she wanted to look away. "Justin, your son is fine, but he's being admitted to the NICU for a course of antibiotics."

Her professional exterior fractured when she turned to the Jorgensons.

Katherine stood, pulling Martin up with her. "Isaiah's sick?"

"He doesn't appear to be," Priya answered. "He'll be monitored and have to stay admitted for the course of his antibiotics." She swallowed hard. Her eyes brimmed with tears that spilled down her cheeks. "I'm so sorry. Maisy didn't make it."

Katherine collapsed into Martin's arms. They both sank to the floor.

Numbness crept over Justin's body. Maisy was gone. Just like that. She'd never see their son. She'd never rock him to sleep. And she wouldn't be there to raise him.

A warm hand gripped his arm. Priya. She'd been a lifeline through this drama. An old friend from high school, the calm and collected doctor, the voice of reason that kept Maisy from ruining her own life as she meddled in his.

"Go in. The nurses will direct you where to go." She glanced at Maisy's parents. "I'll bring them back when they're ready."

He should stay. But while these parents had just lost their child, there was a child who had yet to meet his own parent.

Justin passed through the door. Faceless, nameless people in scrubs directed him in his daze until he was in front of a large set of windows overlooking a few scary contraptions that resembled plastic cages. One was surrounded by staff. He could barely make out the wiggling baby inside.

Isaiah. Isaiah Martin to be exact. The Jorgensons had lost Maisy. Justin wasn't going to change their grandson's entire name. But Isaiah's last name would be Walker now. It'd be easier, since he would be raising the boy. That'd been a conflict he'd been prepared to lose. Now it was a given. He felt no satisfaction at the victory.

A nurse popped out and walked him through the process of scrubbing in to go inside the NICU. Once he was soaped, rinsed, and dried, she led him inside. She rambled off details about how Isaiah should be able to stay in Moore since he was a healthy, full-term baby. If he were to get sick like Maisy, they'd transport him to a bigger hospital. But his boy had to go through a full round of treatment before he could go home. To Justin's home.

Isaiah would stay with him.

Isaiah would stay. With him. Forever.

He stopped in front of the incubator they had Isaiah in. The nurse rattled off more instructions. He'd have to ask later what the hell she'd said.

As he gazed at a perfect little body and the cries reached his ears, he couldn't pull himself out of his thoughts. He wasn't just hanging around to help Maisy with his son and fight for every visit he could get. He was *raising* his son. Intuition told him that Maisy's parents wouldn't fight him. At least not initially. They had a daughter to bury. But he'd have to have a tough discussion with them about their expectations for their grandson. Sooner rather than later.

He reached through the circular door of the incubator and threaded a finger through Isaiah's five perfect little digits. Wires were attached to his son's chest and a line went through his umbilical stump. The tiniest diaper Justin had even seen wound around him.

The nurse was talking feedings now, but Justin wasn't listening.

You and me, big guy. We're going to get through this together.

CHAPTER 2

*H*er bedroom was dark. Quiet. Priya sat on the edge of her bed in her pajamas. The silk bottoms matched her camisole top. She'd managed to dress the part of a stable adult, but her clothing didn't match her state of mind. Mismatched. Distracted. Darting.

Maisy was gone. Her best friend. Though that status had been questionable ever since Priya had moved home to work at her dad's clinic. The ten years she'd been away had felt like twenty-five when she hung out with Maisy. After her friend had gotten pregnant, their relationship had turned more professional and less personal.

What Maisy had done was unconscionable. Lying about being on birth control was ugly, and giving Justin a condom that was well past its expiration date had only compounded the deception. But then the way she'd tried to manipulate Justin with the baby? That had been despicable. But Maisy had been in a bad place mentally, and Priya hadn't had the heart to cut the woman completely out of her life. They'd stayed together for the same reason they'd been attached at the hip in high school: no one else understood them.

Priya with her social shyness and aspirations for an Ivy League medical school. A willingness to devote her free time to studying and activities that'd make her application shine. Debate team. Volunteer work. Part-time work at the hospital.

Then there'd been Maisy and her mood swings that drove away anyone who got close to her. Except for Priya. Priya's straitlaced personality hadn't been a deal breaker. No, instead it had been a reason Maisy could feel better about herself. She was the older, wiser wild child to Priya's studious innocent.

It had worked then. At almost thirty, it had failed to stand the test of time.

But now it didn't matter. Maisy was gone.

Priya sighed and let her head fall back, staring at her white ceiling. "Why didn't you just go to the doctor, Maise?"

She knew the answer without needing a reply from the great beyond. Maisy's parents had urged her to go to the clinic, and that had been enough to make her stay home. Normally, it would've been fine. Priya could've even recommended an over-the-counter medicine. Maisy had been far enough along. But this infection had been different. Unusual, but not rare enough for Priya to write a medical paper on it. Not that she would. Not for a case that still gave her restless "what could I have done better" nights a month later.

Her friend just lying there in the surgical suite. As pale as the white blanket she'd been draped in. So still.

Priya shook herself. Her first year out of residency, and she'd lost a patient. The image was one she'd have to live with. Her instructors always said that if she had a long and prosperous career, no matter how successful, losing a patient would be inevitable.

She thought back on her career trajectory. All those nights studying to finish college early. Attacking med school admission to get into Stanford—and making it on her first try. And coming home to work in a rural hospital and give back to the world for all her good fortune.

All that, and she couldn't save a girl she'd known better than anyone. Maisy should be here with her own son. She should be learning life's lessons through raising her kid. She shouldn't have died.

Priya blinked back tears but failed to stop the trail they left down her cheeks. If she'd been a better friend and a better doctor, maybe Maisy would still be here.

She wept quietly. Living with her parents while she got settled was a blessing and a curse. Her dad was a doctor in town and pushing close to retirement. Her mom was a nurse, one he'd met during his own residency. Mom had been born and raised in Moore. Dad had followed her back home.

Together, they were a well of support and understanding without stifling her. Though right now, she could do with a little stifling. Some concerned glances. A few more questions, like *"How are you doing?"* But they reserved all their parental concern for her younger sister, Devya, as she traipsed across France in the name of art.

A buzzing sound filled the silence. Her phone. She wasn't on call and it was after eleven at night.

Justin's name popped up.

She'd wrapped her own turmoil in a tidy package when she was around him in the hospital and at the funeral. The magnitude of being a single dad and losing someone he'd known his whole life had hit him like a raging bull. Flattened him. Each day she was on rounds, she'd sought him out in the NICU. Each day of the two weeks Isaiah had been admitted, Justin had been there, holding Isaiah's tiny hand or foot or sometimes rocking the baby in a chair by the isolette.

Isaiah had been released a couple weeks ago, and she missed those morning chats. Two friends talking about everything other than what had happened. But those moments had made her feel better.

She answered her phone, speaking low though her parents' room was situated across the house. "Is everything okay?"

What if he asked her the same question? How would she answer? The temptation to overmedicate every mom who complained of a cough or fatigue hounded her. She second-guessed every decision and stayed late after work checking up on patients. She was becoming a helicopter OB and it'd burn her out in no time if she didn't get her act together.

"Sorry to bother you." She fluttered her eyes closed at the deep rumble on the other end of the line. The secret crush she'd nursed since middle school never failed to resurface at the most inappropriate times. Like when Maisy had squeed that he was back in town and had finally returned one of her calls. Or when his face had filled with awe and wonder during the very first prenatal ultrasound.

The way she'd just wanted him to hold her and tell her everything would be okay after she'd delivered the healthy baby of her dying friend.

Her feelings shamed her. He was the one who needed the support. And like all the other times, she had to be the responsible one. The strong one. Always the smarty-pants who knew what to do.

She got out of her head long enough to hear the faint squalling of a baby. Powerful lungs for a little guy. "What's wrong?"

His words rushed over the phone like the wind blowing outside her window. "He's not sleeping. And he cries all the time. The last two nights, it's like the clock hits eight and a switch flips. He cries for hours. Screams. What am I doing wrong? Is he sick? Is he—"

"Relax, Justin. Where is he now?" She had zero worries

about Isaiah's safety in his dad's care, unlike the lingering doubts she'd harbored about the boy's mom.

"Up in his crib so I could call and hear you. Mom and Dad left last week and I— *Fuck*. I don't know what I'm doing."

The urge to chuckle was strong, but she bit her lip. Now wasn't the time. He was a dad going out of his mind with worry, and this situation was so *normal*. But it was only refreshing for her. "Most first-time parents feel that way." Her father had gotten these panicked calls when she was a kid. "Is he still eating okay and dirtying diapers throughout the day?"

"The kid shits more than any ranch animal I've been around." A heavy sigh floated over the phone. He was calming down.

"Then my unofficial observation would be colic. He's in the timeline for when it starts."

"What the fuck is colic? Hold on, I should check on him. No, I can't keep you on the line. I— Dammit. I don't know what to do."

Cool, collected Justin was harried and unsure of himself. This was a side of him she'd never seen. Most of her high school years had been spent being the third wheel with him and Maisy.

"Want me to come over?" The offer slipped out before she could think too hard about it. She had work in the morning and she wouldn't do this for a patient. Too many lines crossed. But he was a friend. And he'd turned to her when she felt less than worthy.

A couple of heartbeats went by. "Could you?" The hopefulness and yearning in his voice clinched her decision.

"I'll be right there."

"God, thank you."

She clicked off and looked down at herself. It wouldn't make sense to change into nice clothes to go rock a baby.

Unless she was in scrubs for surgery, no one saw her this casual. Ever. Especially not Justin. She combed out her hair and changed into a pair of knit leggings and a cowl-neck sweater.

Her parents were in bed but probably not asleep. She sent them a message telling them she was meeting a friend. They wouldn't ask questions. They never did about her personal life. School, yes. Residency, yes. But not boyfriends or how she was doing after Emmett had dropped her after residency. They hadn't even asked why.

But that was for the best. Priya relived the breakup often enough; at least she didn't have to share it.

The night was dark and chilly. Fresh lake scents surrounded her, the fishy tang of middle summer gone. A crisp wind promised the plummeting temperatures of approaching winter. The smell of earth and pine trees floating on the air was one of her favorite things about living by the lake. The mosquitoes during the summer almost ruined the fun, but the city sprayed heavily. Probably because the city commissioners and other influencers lived in this neighborhood, too.

She parked outside. Her parents had a four-car garage, but aside from their normal vehicles, Dad's sports car took up the third stall. The fourth stall was slotted with their biking gear. Not motorcycles, but bicycles that cost as much as motorcycles and ranged from sturdy mountain bikes to sleek road bikes.

Dad had offered to move them, but since Priya was staying rent-free, she insisted on parking outside. When the temps dipped to twenty below zero in the winter, she might think twice.

She knew the way to Justin's, though she hadn't been there often. In high school, she'd gotten the feeling that Maisy wasn't allowed at his place. Whether that had been a limit Justin set or his mom, Priya didn't know. But it'd been for the best.

Pushing those thoughts to the side, she concentrated on maneuvering out of the lakeside neighborhood where she'd been born and raised. The houses reflected the size of their neighbors' bank accounts, but if they were like her parents, they worked hard for it. Overtime, on-call, and long shifts were her past, present, and future.

But this was going to be her only home visit.

CHAPTER 3

Justin's ears rang, and he was to the point where the screaming had blended into a drone. Isaiah cried and cried. Justin had done the bicycling the legs business that he'd read about when he was still coherent enough to make out words and what they meant. Baby massage had been next. Whatever he did, he'd better not stick a fucking bottle in the kid's mouth. That made him scream harder.

This was the third night since his parents had gone back to Arizona. He hadn't registered more than four total hours of sleep, and if he got a two-hour stretch at one time, it was a damn miracle.

That sleep-when-your-baby-sleeps business was bullshit. Whoever concocted that advice hadn't been a single parent with dishes to wash, laundry, checkups, and a functioning ranch.

Ranchers didn't get maternity leave.

Thank God his sister had moved back to town. Sure, he was happy that Brigit had married his best friend, was blissfully in love, and was happier than he'd ever seen her. But he was selfishly glad that she'd taken over the majority of the sheep-ranching duties until he could come up for air.

When that would be, he had no clue.

Isaiah bunched in his arms and released a wallop of a wail. His tongue was flat, and his little throat had to be raw. The parenting magazines stacked on the end table by the rocking chair said crying didn't hurt babies. Justin had no idea how that could be true. It was hurting him, and he wasn't even the one throwing a fit.

He got up, patting Isaiah's diapered bottom, cradling the boy in the crook of his arm, and wandered around the main floor of his house.

The whole idea that the nursery could be upstairs went down the shitter the second night Isaiah was home—after the fifth trip up and down the stairs.

Why hadn't he cried this much in the nursery?

Priya said colic. He hadn't read up on that yet. He'd seen it mentioned in that strike-fear-in-the-heart-of-new-parents kind of way. But what was it?

And where was Priya?

He did the walk-bounce to the door that was now automatic when he held his son and peered outside. She pulled in and he blew out a gusty breath. She was the calm in the summer hailstorm of his life, but tonight he hadn't trusted calling anyone else. He wanted her opinion. She wasn't a mom herself, but she was a doctor. A doctor whose straight advice and firm instructions he'd used as a lifeline to get him through the idea that he was going to be a dad.

She parked across from his front door, not doing the usual loop around to face out that everyone else did in high school. She hadn't been out here since, and even then, Maisy had preferred to stay away if his parents were home. Mom and Dad had preferred it that way, too.

He flipped the porch light on. Priya shut her door and

glanced over. The lift of her brows was clear in the glow of his yard light. Yeah, Isaiah's screaming was that loud.

"Hi," he said as he held the door open for her. For the first time since his parents had boarded the flight to Phoenix, he felt like he might survive this infant phase.

She smiled, inspecting him closer than Isaiah. He must look a mess. Gone were the suits of his corporate days, and even the neatly trimmed hair he'd kept up since moving home wasn't happening anymore. He had a good week of beard growth, shaggy hair that was probably sticking out to the four winds, and plaid pajama pants with a fresh-ish blue T-shirt. A burp rag dotted with green turtles hung over his right shoulder. He'd learned the hard way to always have one ready.

While Priya always looked good, tonight she was an angel in front of him. Her sleek hair was piled over one shoulder. The long sweater she wore did nothing to hide her ample curves, and if it had, those forest-green leggings would have spilled the secret that she had an incredible body anyway.

"How are you doing, Justin?" He couldn't tell if she'd spoken up or if reading lips was a new talent he'd developed. She didn't wait for an answer. After she stepped out of boots fancier than this farm had ever seen, she gently pried Isaiah from his grip. "Let me peek at him, and if everything's okay, I'll take over and you can get some rest."

He wanted to laugh at the absurdity of sleeping through this noise. His logical brain, the deeply buried portion that used to close multimillion-dollar deals, said he had to try. But the parental instinct was strong. He was too attuned to his son. How could he drift off when there was nowhere in the house where he could hide from the crying?

Seeing his son in Priya's capable hands eased a part of him that was coiled so tight. His mom was good with the baby, but she wasn't a doctor. Priya had said several times that she wasn't a family doctor or pediatrician, but he didn't care. She had medical training and liked babies enough to help them enter the world.

She was cooing as she checked him over. "You're just all a fuss, aren't you? Giving Daddy a hard time."

Isaiah had shushed at the new voice, but his volume was now ratcheting up again. Justin drifted closer, needing Priya's comfort more than Isaiah.

"Is he okay?"

"Healthy as a..." Her lips curved. "Ram."

A grudging smile tugged at his lips. He was a sheep rancher. That was what he'd always liked about her. She paid attention. She knew about his life and seemed to genuinely care about it. A breath of fresh air after the last couple of women in his life.

His ex, the one who had made him bitter enough to call Maisy a year ago, wasn't mentally unstable like Maisy. She was calculating. A damn Jedi master at manipulation. Maisy's actions had seemed comical after the way Gabrielle had screwed him over. But he had to give Gabrielle one thing: she never would've used a baby as a power play. In contrast, after one broken condom, Maisy had proved that she suffered from some undiagnosed mental disorder.

Now both women seemed like figments from another life. Both were lost to him in different ways. He had his son, who deserved all of his attention and best efforts. That, he was sure of. Just like he was 100 percent certain that he was done with women and the games they played.

JUSTIN LOOKED like hell and it wasn't fair how handsome he still was.

Priya swaddled Isaiah, doing her best to secure him as

snugly as possible. She'd reviewed all the education she'd had on colic and tried to recall every mom who lamented about the hard days and longer nights of raising a baby with it. She liked to think that one of the signs she was maturing as a doctor was that she listened and learned from those stories as much as from her teachers. She was focused on women's health and not infant health, but Isaiah seemed healthy.

It was time to deal with the dad. The dad with the sinful stubble that looked better than when he was clean-shaven.

Since she'd moved home, he always seemed to have a few days of growth darkening his face and deepening the blue of his eyes. The contrast with his dirty-blond hair was intriguing and something she thought about way too much. His loose pants hung low on his hips and his lean muscles were too apparent through the thin material of his shirt. She'd be tempted to drool if the dark circles under his eyes and the hang of his shoulders didn't snap her back to reality. A reality in which he was not just her best friend's ex, but the ex of a friend who had recently died—under her care.

Tonight was about Justin, not her unresolved feelings for him. "Go lay down," she said in her best authoritative tone, the one she used in the surgery suite. "I've got him."

His look was a strange mix of hopeful, relieved, and terrified. "I don't think I can."

He'd better. Isaiah's screaming wasn't going anywhere and if the baby had colic, then this was Justin's life until it passed.

"Doctor's orders." She waved him off.

The corner of his mouth hitched up, and he shuffled to a short hallway that must house the door to his bedroom. He stopped and glanced over his shoulder. "Formula and bottles are by the sink. We have rural water, but it tastes weird without being filtered. There's a water jug next to the can of formula."

She nodded, uncertainty trickling in. How would she know if Isaiah was hungry? Her training came back to her. Rooting. Right. But in the throws of colic, he probably wasn't going to eat anything.

"Where's the nursery?" she asked before he disappeared completely.

"Upstairs."

Perfect. The distance would muffle the cries. If she were more comfortable driving through the county in the dark, she'd load Isaiah's car seat and go for a long drive. Maybe next time.

She paused and looked up the stairs. Who said there'd be a next time?

But come on. The guy was alone with a baby with colic. Last year, she'd had a mom break down with sobs that shook her body. She'd cried so hard, Priya had worried she'd upset her C-section healing even after six weeks. The poor thing had been facing the end of her maternity leave and her baby had been like Isaiah since week three.

Okay, so there'd be a next time. And she'd bring earplugs. The nursery was quiet and—

Wow. Not the nursery she'd expected, but then Justin hadn't planned on being allowed much access to his own kid.

The decor was done in earth tones, complete with framed artwork of various countryside views. The carpet was whitish, but she didn't dare flip on the light to check. The less she stimulated Isaiah the better.

A crib was on one side of the room. The wall above it was bare. She smiled. The fear of a heavy picture dropping into the crib must've chased the decoration away.

Smart move.

Next to the crib was a changing table. Diapers spilled from a box next to the table, and across from those was a dresser. Tiny little clothes were probably folded inside.

She scanned the mess of diapers, the wipes package that was hanging open, the pile of unopened baby gifts nestled under the window.

The clothes may not be neatly folded inside.

Was Justin the type to be bothered by the clutter? She didn't know.

She was the type to be bothered by the clutter. Arranging Isaiah in a cradle hold, she squatted and neatly piled the diapers. Then she closed the wipes. Her fingers itched to open the drawers, but now wasn't the time.

A red light from the baby monitor shone next to the changing table.

She leaned down to murmur into it. "Get some rest, Justin." Clicking the monitor off, she lowered herself into the plush rocking chair and kicked her feet up.

"All right, baby. Give your daddy a break." She sighed and settled in the rocking chair with Isaiah still in the crook of her arm. If she cradled him against her chest, he tried to throw himself around. A strong kid already.

Isaiah.

In her office, Justin had commented that he and Maisy hadn't settled on a name. Priya had known exactly what Maisy was going to name her son, but she'd also known that if she mentioned it, Maisy would find another doctor and cut Priya out of her life.

By then, Priya hadn't considered herself close to Maisy anymore. Like Justin, she'd just been in it for the baby. Unlike Justin, she hadn't been able to discuss many of her concerns with him. Doctor-patient confidentiality. Maisy's actions had been questionable even before pregnancy, but she hadn't weathered the hormones well.

Isaiah Martin Walker.

Maisy's parents probably hadn't liked losing the last name. Or maybe they hadn't cared. She hadn't braved a visit with them. If she had a hard time not blaming herself, what did they think? She was afraid to know. In school, they'd loved her and Maisy as friends. It was like they'd hoped her deep sense of responsibility would rub off on Maisy. Did they think she'd failed their daughter as an adult?

It wasn't time for her pain. Justin was a stand-up guy and the father, and she couldn't see them pointing the finger at him.

How much had they worried about Maisy's mental health? Or had they thought that since Maisy was hanging with Priya again, she'd take care of it?

Her musings had a muting effect on the crying. She gazed down at her bundle. Isaiah's wails were pretty steady. His little hands in fists, his mouth open. Cute guy. Loud.

There wasn't much else to do but rock him. She dug her phone out of her pocket and looked at her emails, social medias sites, and ugh, the time. She had to work in the morning.

But tomorrow wasn't a surgery day. She wasn't on call. And she had extra scrubs in the office. Her coworkers might wonder at her wearing scrubs in the clinic, but she doubted anyone would question her.

Setting an alarm, she renewed her determination to stick it out for the long haul.

Why?

Why was she here, doing this for Justin?

They were friends, yes, but it wasn't like they called each other when they were back in town. They didn't email, send memes back and forth, or hang out. Justin wasn't a social media guy. Maisy had been the glue that stuck them together.

How had she forgiven Maisy in the first place? The girl had known Priya crushed so hard on Justin when they were in middle school. Next thing Priya knew, Maisy was biting her lip and whispering, spilling details about making out with him in tenth grade after the last football game of the year. Priya should've made her move by then, but she hadn't been willing to sacrifice her GPA for a boy.

She blew out a puff of air and shifted Isaiah to her other arm. The real reason she'd never made a move? Justin had never looked at her any differently than any other girl in school. He was congenial and friendly with everyone. She wasn't special.

And wasn't that the rub.

The child of a busy doctor and nurse wanted to feel special for more than her academic skills. Surprise. Her sister had gotten all that attention.

The day when Maisy gushed about Justin's skills with French kissing, Priya wrote him off. She deserved better. But she hadn't gotten "better" when it came to relationships. Just more selfish men.

Didn't mean she didn't sneak a glimpse of Justin's jean-clad ass when she could. Or notice how wide his shoulders were. And she knew that he was eight inches taller than her.

Glutton for punishment, party of one?

She let her eyes drift shut and rocked a still-crying Isaiah. Yeah. She noticed too much about the rancher, and this wasn't the time.

CHAPTER 4

*J*ustin flipped his eyes open. The house was quiet; Isaiah must be sleeping.

The only sound was the wind blowing outside and the branches scraping against the side of the house. How long had he slept?

It was almost morning. Was Priya still here?

Rolling up to a sitting position, he ran his hands through his hair. Damn, he needed a trim. For three weeks, they'd been doing this. When she wasn't on call—hell, even when she was on call—she would come over and help him with Isaiah. There was no way Justin could pay her back. She had saved his sanity in so many ways, and she never asked for anything.

They didn't have much time to talk. She relieved him so he could rest while she retreated to the nursery. She took half the night shift, and some mornings; by the time he woke, she'd switched the monitor on and was gone.

Shoving to his feet, he padded out of his room and up the stairs. Instead of going into the nursery, he walked to the window at the end of the hall. Autumn in Minnesota could be unpredictable. One day could be sunny and forty-five degrees, and the next could be a full-on blizzard. A lifetime of farming and ranching meant he kept his ear peeled for news about what was going on in the weather world. On the news last night—with the captions on because he couldn't hear a word over Isaiah's screaming—they'd predicted freezing rain.

Priya also lived out of town in that fancy little residential area off the lakeshore, but she wasn't used to driving on gravel. Ice could make that slippery, too.

His yard didn't look bad but above the trees it was hazy. Drizzly. The temperature at night had dipped below freezing. He went to the nursery and pushed open the door. Peeking inside, his gaze went directly to the swaddled little bundle in the middle of the crib. Isaiah was slumbering peacefully, his breaths even and soft.

Next, he sought out Priya. Her midnight-black hair hung over one shoulder and her head rested on her curled fist. She had her legs stretched out on the footrest and was fast asleep.

She never went to the neighboring room to stretch out on the bed, instead curling up in the rocking chair like she'd rather be close if Isaiah needed anything. And it usually meant more sleep for him. He didn't understand it. She had a challenging job, a demanding one. But she was here in the middle of the night, looking out for him.

He hated to wake her up but the last few mornings she'd almost slept in and missed work. Her alarm was set too low to wake her up after being busy half the night with a colicky baby.

Justin took one more second to look her over. She was dressed like she could open her eyes and go right to work. She was never anything less than put together and professional. Of course the night Isaiah was born, at the hospital, she'd been in scrubs, but he hadn't noticed much more than the expression on her face. In the clinic, she wore business clothing under her lab coat. And it was business *formal* clothing, not business casual. She'd even been like that while they were in school.

He used to be, too, once. A span of his life he didn't remember fondly. It was almost laughable to think that his coworkers in Denver would never recognize him if they passed him on the street now. Thanks to Gabrielle, his transition had started in college, and thanks to Gabrielle, his regression had started as soon as he'd moved home. And he didn't miss it one bit.

He tiptoed over to Priya and crouched down. His gaze caught on the changing table. The diapers were piled in a neat stack. He bet if he opened the dresser drawer, he'd find yesterday's laundry refolded and organized.

A smile ghosted over his lips and he looked back at Priya. The urge to steal a peaceful minute to watch her sleep was strong, but also…wrong. His mind flashed to the night in the hospital and the dark circles under her eyes, the weight of his world on her shoulders while she stood strong and performed her job, despite her own hurting.

No, he shouldn't be looking at her like this.

Her eyes fluttered open, and he missed their brilliant brown in the dim room. She had amazing eyes, like those polished tiger-eye stones he used to see in souvenir shops as a kid.

They stared at each other for a heartbeat before he spoke. "The roads might be crap. I don't want you to have to rush."

Her forehead furrowed as she tried to wake up. "Work. Right." Her voice was sleep-roughened; husky. He shouldn't have noticed, shouldn't be hoping she'd keep talking, but he hadn't been with a woman since Maisy had gotten pregnant.

Did bachelors celebrate one-year abstinence anniversaries?

Ones who had been so epically screwed by women did.

He rose and kept his voice low. "I know you have a full day of patients."

Her expression flickered so fast he couldn't read it. Then she tipped her head toward the crib. "I fed him at three. He seems to be ready to sleep the day away."

She'd been doing that, covering his feedings after the witching hours passed. Her generosity granted him an extra few hours of uninterrupted, deep sleep. With her efforts, he could make it through the day without feeling like he was losing his mind. He even tossed a load of clothes in the wash or did dishes instead of collapsing in a chair with a baby on his chest.

She got up and stretched.

Don't look. Don't look. He couldn't watch those curvy legs of hers go taut. And the way she gripped her sleeves in her palms as she reached her arms above her head was too fucking adorable.

This was Priya. He didn't get lewd thoughts about her. She'd been his girlfriend's friend; now she was his. It hadn't been allowed even before he'd cut himself off from dating.

He snuck out of the nursery first, not trusting himself to avoid checking out her ass. Those thick sweaters she wore weren't enough to hide the sway of her hips.

Once they hit the bottom of the stairs, she leaned in and he automatically drifted toward her. "Are you going to try it? The baby sling," she whispered.

Oh. That.

When she'd arrived last night and lifted that gauzy fabric from her tote, his mind had defaulted to wicked thoughts and images. And questions. Like was her skin as soft as it looked? And if she were encased by the dark blue material and nothing else, would it make her complexion glow, or chafe? He didn't like the idea of the material marring her in any way.

When she'd wrapped it around her back and shoulders, he'd almost choked on the surge of lust that slammed into him. Then she'd started saying thing like "wearing" and "baby" in the same sentence and reality had smacked him upside the head.

She thought it'd be a good idea for him to cocoon Isaiah in that thing and wander around like one of his ewes with a suckling lamb.

Fuck. No.

His face must've revealed the answer. He didn't plan on touching the wrap.

"Well there's a brochure if you're interested," she said, shrugging into a puffy white coat that swallowed her whole. "My nurse, Krista, teaches workshops on baby wearing so if you have any questions, I can ask her."

"Did you have to buy that thing?" It looked like a death trap. How would Isaiah not drop out the bottom? Pop out the top? What if he bent to pick something up and the baby spilled out? He had enough stress without dropping babies on their heads.

But Priya had helped him so much the last couple of weeks, he couldn't ignore her gesture. He'd asked for her help because he trusted her with Isaiah. Maybe it wouldn't hurt to...wear his baby?

Her lips twitched at his tone. He jerked his gaze away before she could catch him staring at her mouth. He'd just been waiting for her full smile, but... Though he'd pulled himself off the market long ago, he wasn't prepared for the hard work of ignoring his body's demand.

All he had to do was remember why he'd moved home in the first place. His gaze strayed to the pile of fabric on the edge of the couch. If he wanted to get laid, he'd probably have to wait until his son went off to college.

Wiping all thoughts of sex out of his mind, he shoved his hands in the pockets of his flannel sweatpants. Sex should be the farthest thing from his mind. The last few weeks, he'd smelled of baby powder and sour milk. The diaper bin was noxious, and he hadn't shaved in almost two months.

Real man candy. But the last thing he wanted to do was scare off Priya. He wasn't going to be the guy who went after his dead ex-girlfriend's best friend. Being with Priya would be poor taste under other circumstances, but the tragic baggage made it worse.

Besides, even if she'd ever be interested in this lifetime, how would it look if he made a move on his late ex's best friend? What would Priya think of him? He couldn't risk his friendship with her, or the trust he had in her abilities. That trust didn't extend to relationships.

KRISTA SIDLED up next to her and leaned against the counter. She plopped a white Styrofoam cup of green tea next to Priya's work laptop. "So. Was he open to the idea?"

The "he" in question flashed through Priya's mind. She'd woken up to him crouched in front of her, all angles and shadows, his warm and comforting presence blending into the soothing ambiance of the nursery. The room had a different feel than the rest of the house. Time stalled when she walked in. Her worries were left outside the doorway and all she had to worry about was Isaiah, not how his mommy would never see him smile or grow up. Or her conflicting feelings about his daddy. Just a crying baby who settled down after a few hours, slept, and took a bottle like a champ.

As for Krista's question… Her lips twitched as she recalled Justin's furrowed brow and dubious expression while she unraveled the baby wrap. "I think necessity might dictate how open he is."

Krista snickered. "Once he discovers how freeing it is, he'll think marsupials are geniuses. I still get a lot of resistance from mommies, but I've taught several dads baby wearing."

"I plan to hit him up again when I go there tonight."

Sympathy welled in Krista's face. "Still battling the colic?"

She nodded, her carefully pinned bun not moving a hair. This morning she'd been so tired she'd almost just worn a ponytail. But it was hard enough getting taken seriously as *the* Dr. Patel's daughter. People in Moore were just getting accustomed to doctors who hadn't been practicing in town for decades and doctors who weren't several years older than them.

At least Priya had chosen a good field. Her age wasn't as much of a concern as long as she had good word of mouth. But the spattering of cancellations since Maisy's death had stung—and reinforced that little voice at the back of her head that told her she wasn't enough.

You're just…you. Not that that's bad. But I want more. Excitement. In and out of the bedroom.

Her cheeks burned. Emmett's words were branded into her mind. She didn't have true OCD, but she liked a clean environment. If she changed sheets, or didn't want to slam body fluids together over material that couldn't be tossed in a washing machine, was that so wrong? She didn't have to stop and warn company, "Watch out for that stain on the couch. I orgasmed all over it."

She grabbed a cleaning wipe from the container she always kept on her desk. Dabbing at her laptop, she mentally thanked the clinic administrator all over again for pairing her with Krista. Her nurse was a walking no-judg-ment zone.

Krista checked her watch. "Our one o'clock canceled if you need to grab a little shut-eye. Libby Delano."

Priya jerked her head up. Libby had canceled? She'd been one of her first appointments. Libby had walked in and announced, "So glad to finally have a girl doctor in town to look under the hood. And one who won't make weird comments about my child-bearing hips."

Yes, Dr. Jameson had retired a couple of years ago, leaving the town sorely deficient in female physicians for any appointments related to women's health. Dr. Bezos was in his late fifties and had been practicing in Moore since he'd gotten out of med school, much like Priya.

But he rubbed Priya the wrong way. A little condescend-ing, a touch dismissive, always a hint of a sneer when she discussed patient issues with him. Her residency had been in a supportive environment, the experienced doctors mentoring the new physicians. In Moore, Priya was starting to feel like she'd settled into a canoe that someone had booted out into the current. That someone was Dr. Bezos.

Krista nudged her with an elbow. "Relax, Doc. She said she wants her family doctor to deliver the baby. Start from the very beginning."

"Right." Priya couldn't bring herself to believe it. Libby was due in less than three months. Priya had been the one to confirm the pregnancy, she'd celebrated the gender reveal, and she'd talked Libby through glucose testing when the first-time mom's nerves were about to implode. "Any more cancellations?"

"Only, um…"

"It's okay, Krista. I'm a big girl." Only she didn't feel like it today. The first place she wanted to go was to her dad's office. At home, Mom and Dad didn't act like they'd heard anything. She didn't want to bother them. They'd probably tell her all new doctors had unpredictable schedules until they built their client base.

"The C-section scheduled for Monday."

"Michelle Little Deer?" But Michelle had sat in her office three weeks ago and outlined her exact plans for the surgery. Her husband would sit in. He'd be the first to hold the baby after Priya's team checked the infant over. Then he and the baby would stay by Michelle's side until she was stitched up.

Michelle was so earnest and excited that Priya had felt like an honored part of the baby team.

"Yeah," Krista said gently. "She's afraid of infection and all that and is going to the city to give birth."

She was afraid of what had killed Maisy? But each surgery suite was meticulously cleaned, and every person involved in the procedure painstakingly scrubbed in.

Or was Michelle afraid of who was doing the surgery?

"Light afternoon, then?" It'd give Priya a chance to catch up on…feeling sorry for herself. There were always reports to finish—except she was caught up.

Krista only mentioned the cancellations. But her calendar was growing increasingly bare, too. And not just from women having babies. Current patients weren't booking out annual physicals after they left her office. The chronic cases she was overseeing had left to seek second opinions. Priya advocated and supported second opinions, but in this case, that wasn't what was happening.

They no longer trusted her.

"Light afternoon. Enjoy it while it lasts." Krista bobbed away, her ponytail swinging. How long before she found a position with a busier doctor?

How long before Priya lost her job because she wasn't bringing clients in?

CHAPTER 5

The oven timer was going off. The dryer was buzzing. And Isaiah was fussing.

At least he wasn't outright crying.

Eyeballing the swatch of material he was supposed to somehow harness Isaiah in, Justin picked his son up and tucked him into a football hold.

It was feeding time, but he just had to rotate laundry so Isaiah had a clean sleeper for tonight. And take the tater tots and chicken strips out of the oven. He spun away from the laundry room. The food was first. He didn't need burned tots, nor did he need smoke alarms going off.

In the kitchen, he glanced around, knowing full well there was no good place to set a baby down. Isaiah was too young for a high chair and Justin didn't even own one. He went back out to the living room, set his son on the carpet, and jogged back to the kitchen.

As he took out supper, his stomach clenched so hard. All those high-end meals at world-renowned restaurants and he was having dump 'n' serve. How far he'd fallen—or been pushed, as he thought about it.

Enough self-pity. He was happier ranching. The whole marketing gig hadn't been his first life plan anyway. That had been ranching—until his dad and uncles had sold the family farm and ranch operation to Travis and his cousins. It was one thing to grow up knowing the plan was to sell the farm and ranch to Travis, but when the sale had actually gone through? He'd been left with the *now whats.*

It wasn't that long ago, but it was before his cousins' wives and kids had come along. The Walker clan hadn't needed Justin's help, and his own parents had treated him like he was free to go out and conquer the world. So he had tried. In college, he'd clicked so well with Gabrielle, and they'd had big plans…

Isaiah let out a cry.

Justin dropped the pot holder and scratched his head. From where he stood, he could see out to where Isaiah was wiggling on the floor. Should he make a bottle while he was in here, or get the wash into the dryer first?

Isaiah's wails grew. Justin winced. He had a predictable night full of hollering ahead. *Please don't start now.*

"Hey," Priya called from the entry. Her voice dropped as she cooed to the squawking baby. "Who's a good little boy?"

Yes, his savior was here. He rushed out, and not for the first time, he wished he were wearing something other than pajama pants and an old T-shirt. They were clean. Fairly clean. No, they needed to be thrown in the wash.

"Hey," he called back, his raised voice quieting Isaiah. "Ready to get your world rocked by tater tots and chicken strips?"

Her chuckle drifted in ahead of her. He grinned—until he saw her. Her shoulders hung like she'd lost the big game, her face was drawn, and her smile was wan. She had been getting less sleep than him, and not in her own bed.

She had Isaiah in her arms. He held his hands out to take the baby.

"As long as there's ketchup, I'll just have tater tots," she said, going straight for the bottles. Isaiah had gone back to his *I'm hungry* cries.

"You're going to miss out on processed meat?"

"I hate to confess to a rancher that I'm a vegetarian. It was my dad's thing." She lifted her hands like *Whaddya know?* "Had to be like Dad."

"Your dad's a vegetarian and his in-laws own a butcher shop?"

She rinsed off a dishcloth and wiped down the counter from end to end. It wasn't *that* dirty, but she did it. Every time. "I think he's a vegetarian *because* of Grandpa Saunders. They get along now, but it was a little rocky at first. You know, city boy meeting the country girl's parents. Different political views, different worldly opinions. Holidays were a good time."

"Impressive passive-aggressive move. What do your grandparents think about you being a vegetarian?"

He couldn't see her expression as she measured out formula and water, but her shoulders tightened. "They don't really... I... They're so busy, I don't see them a lot, unless I stop in at the shop. I think since I'm willing to walk around a raw meat buffet, they aren't insulted by it."

He hadn't known that about her. Or them. An insatiable well of curiosity yawned open. They'd gone to school together. She hadn't played sports. She was wicked smart. She apparently preferred a clean and organized environment. That wasn't much to know about someone he'd spent so much time with.

He didn't have a chance to ask any more questions. She shook the bottle and turned around. Her gaze stopped on the pan of tots and strips. "Did you cook like that before?"

He propped Isaiah on his shoulder and was promptly nuzzled by a baby rooting for milk. "No. I ate out—or shamelessly waited for Caleb to make something when he lived here."

He hadn't just eaten out. He'd been a fine-dining snob. The best steak houses in Denver. When he flew out of the country for work, his free time was filled with trendy restaurants and meals that came in multiple courses on fancy plates. Meals that boasted local ingredients that somehow boosted the price.

Some places in Moore served good enough food, but it'd clog an artery more than tease his taste buds. It was probably better than what he'd pulled out of the oven, but at least he didn't have to worry about a crying baby in a restaurant.

She took Isaiah from him. "Take a breather."

"You've been working all day."

A shadow crossed her face. "It's fine. It was a light day."

"What's wrong?" He didn't miss that she carefully altered her expression to look mildly surprised. "Don't try to hide it. You and I are battle buddies."

"Just the normal stuff." And there it was again. The hopelessness of someone with water closing over their head and no swimming skills.

"And normal stuff is that bad?"

"It gets to me. Young and inexperienced, I guess." She gave Isaiah his bottle and wandered out of the kitchen. "I'll get through it."

He couldn't pinpoint how he knew she was lying, but there was more to the story. Yet she was done talking about it, and that bruised his ego. They were friends. They'd been through a lot together the last few months. The last year. While they may not have spoken directly, their eye communication had been next level.

Maisy would turn to him and say, "Did you hear that,

Justin? You can stay over in the hospital room with me as long as I'm in."

Priya would look over Maisy's shoulder at him, her eyes saying, *"It's a good idea not to leave her alone with the baby, but don't for one second think she won't use this to control you."*

Then when Maisy turned back to her, he'd give Priya a look that said, *"I know she's going to take advantage of it, but what can I do?"*

Then there were the times Priya had been at Maisy's place right after the pregnancy announcement. He'd shoot her a *"Has she always been like this?"* expression, and she'd return it with a shake of her head, her dark eyes saying, *"She's getting worse."*

Something was bothering Priya. Did he press her? His gut told him no. If it was about her job, she had parents in the field who were much better equipped to understand her situation.

Instead, he fixed her a plate, added extra ketchup, and carried it out to her. Her wooden stare was directed at the far wall as Isaiah gurgled with his bottle. Whatever had happened today wasn't an ordinary work situation.

He set the plate on the end table next to the recliner. "Finger good. Good for eating one-handed."

She glanced up, the glassiness back in her eyes. "Oh, thank you."

He waited for a heartbeat, but she didn't say more. A frustrating quality now that he was on the other end. He'd never been one to talk about his personal life. But then, he hadn't had much to be truly proud of. His former life had all been a puppet show—and he'd been the puppet. "You mind if I grab a shower after I do laundry?"

Her attention was back on the wall. "Not at all."

"Okay." He gave her one last look that said, *"I know there's something wrong and I'm right here. Talk to me.*" But she didn't look his way.

"You want to show me how to use that thing later tonight?" He pointed to the baby carrier.

That got a reaction out of her. Her surprise was laced with pleasure. She was happy he was taking her suggestion. "Yeah, sure."

He nodded once and left, planning on a quick shower. There'd be no time to shave—again. The short beard was growing on him, and it was past the scratchy stage,. but he'd at least put on fresh pajama pants. No jeans. He wasn't a glutton for punishment. It was evening, and the colicky hours were approaching.

Tonight, he was learning how to wear his baby, but it wasn't for him. He'd be the star pupil, ask questions, model, whatever it took to get that defeated look out of Priya's eyes.

THE HOTNESS SCALE was burning up.

Justin's hands were on his hips and his shoulders were impossibly wide. Isaiah was swaddled against his chest, the fuzzy top of his head sticking out. The muscles of Justin's forearms were corded, like it was taxing his restraint to keep from wrapping his arms around his baby.

"You want to grab him so bad, don't you?" She laughed, and God, it felt good. Her mouth almost snapped shut, but the temporary release valve for work pressure was too intoxicating. She needed this moment to survive tomorrow and the rest of her days filled with half-empty schedules and canceling patients.

"I really do. I feel like he's going to fall out the bottom."

She tucked her finger around the base of the wrap, failing to ignore how hard Justin's abs were. "Nice and secure. Here.

Feel." She grabbed his hand and placed it where hers was, only she didn't remove her own.

His gaze was distant as he probed the area. It was best he wasn't looking at her as heat wicked up her face.

She moved his hand. "And here." Forcing herself to break contact, she instantly mourned the loss. His hands were surprisingly soft for a guy who worked outside for a living. "You can also keep one hand on him for peace of mind. But it's a good idea to check his position and that his head is still supported. Krista swears up and down that this method is good for newborns, but she wanted me to tell you that there's still a lot of disagreement in the baby-wearing community."

"In other words, do my own research and don't sue her."

Priya giggled again. "You already did the research, didn't you?"

"He fell asleep on me this afternoon but woke up every time I set him in the crib."

"Gotcha. So now when he naps, you can…" She glanced around at the house, and before he could notice her inspection, said, "You can rest."

The mantel and end table needed a good dusting. The kitchen garbage was tied and sitting by the front door. He claimed he couldn't get it into the trash bin, and if he set it on the porch, critters would be attracted to it. Or his dog would get into it. Then there was the clutter. Magazines spilled from the lower shelf of the end table onto the floor. Baby blankets and burp rags were draped over the back of the couch and loveseat. Diapers were piled by each piece of furniture like he changed Isaiah wherever he discovered the boy was wet.

The state of his house wasn't what she was used to. Her parents had built their house after they'd each landed jobs in Moore. It wasn't much older than her, but it was newer than this place. And it'd been updated with the times and remodeled as desired.

Mom had even hired a housekeeper—after Priya left for school. Until then, she'd done the bulk of the cleaning. Devya was the artist. Not expected to hold up her end of the chores, she'd been allowed to be flighty and unreliable.

A beat of jealousy hit her. She busied herself with checking the wrap that went around Justin's back. He bent and gently bounced on the balls of his feet as she did.

She wasn't envious of Devya.

She hadn't been. Until she'd started fearing for her job this morning. If she were let go before her probation was done, would she be able to get another job? Would her parents give her financial support like they did her sister?

Before she knew it, she was stroking her hands along the back of Justin's shoulders, smoothing over the fabric, including some places where there was no baby wrap.

She snatched her hands back. "Sorry. I got lost in my head."

He peered over his shoulder. The move had the unfortunate effect of showing off his strong jaw and long, straight nose. Was it getting hot in here as well? "For a minute there, I wondered if you were going to charge me for the exam," he drawled.

Another laugh burst out of her. "Only the deductible. I'll waive the rest."

"Now, Doc. I keep getting indebted to you."

She folded her arms across herself, afraid she'd touch him again. "You don't owe me. I'm happy to help."

Justin turned to face her. Isaiah's long-distance stare was the one he got as he drifted off, but the wailing would start soon. "I seriously..." He shook his head and looked away. "I don't know what I would've done if you hadn't come every night and Brigit hadn't taken over the ranch."

"That was nice of her."

He snorted, and his grin revealed even, white teeth, his incisors a bit longer than the rest. With his developing beard, he gave off the impression of a dangerous mountain man—in plaid pajama pants and a baby strapped to his chest.

Her heart rate kicked up a few notches.

"It's getting the ranch back from her that'll be the problem." He wandered the living room, testing the wrap as he squatted and bent. This side of Justin was…endearing. A worse threat to her resolve not to crush on him again than his mountain-man appeal.

"She loves it?" Priya didn't know Justin's twin as well as she should for having gone to school with her. Hanging around Maisy had taken care of that. Priya should've realized the extent of the mean-girl tactics, but Maisy hadn't appreciated her chiding and would limit her behavior when Priya was present. And when she wasn't, Priya had tried to help by letting Brigit know what Maisy might target, like clothing out of place or messy hair, but it had only come off as catty and insulting.

If she had a time machine… At least she'd apologized for it. If she had to move away from Moore for work, she wasn't leaving without mending fences.

She nearly giggled at the ranching reference. Perhaps she'd been around Justin too long.

She'd take her chances.

"Bridge loves ranching more than Travis and I." Justin strolled back to her. "He's fallen asleep. Do I dare disrupt his equilibrium and lay him down?"

"Might as well get the night started."

He flashed her another smile before he disappeared upstairs. Collapsing in a chair, she needed a moment to recover from his quick grin.

Her type was not Justin. Sure, she would've been president of his fan club had he not dated Maisy when they were teens. But she still saw other people. Her prom date had been the captain of the speech and debate team. And he'd played chess like a gangster. Then there was Dalton in college. He hadn't tolerated her dedication to studying very well, but he'd gone off to get his PhD in chemistry. Then there was Emmett.

Her whirlwind romance. She'd thought he was the one. But he'd gotten a prestigious fellowship and then outlined how she wasn't enough for him, not professionally and not personally. She'd moved home, refusing to give up her dream of practicing by Dad's side just because some dude with an inflated ego thought it was giving up the game before she lost.

Emmett hadn't felt like some dude at the time.

It wouldn't have been hard for her to move somewhere and start new. Her family wasn't the close-knit unit she'd wanted. Grandma and Grandpa Saunders were tied to their business and had missed all of her graduations after high school. Dad's parents had moved back to London after he was through school, but they were getting older and traveling was too hard. She saw them every few years.

Priya rubbed her temples. Her problem had always been wanting more from her family than they were willing to give. When Mom and Dad weren't working, they liked to travel, and Devya was half a world away. Between grandparents who showed interest in her life but never saw her, and another set who seemed to be okay with not seeing her even though they lived a few miles away, why had she moved back?

"So far, so good." Justin bounded down the stairs. "I can't believe he stayed asleep after I put him down. I thought my heart was going to burst when the door clicked shut."

"Maybe it's a sign he's getting over colic."

He paused at the foot of the stairs and glanced around, a small frown on his face, like this was the first time he'd noticed the state of his surroundings. With a shrug, he pushed a hand through his hair, leaving it sticking up in different directions. Was he not used to longer hair and how it behaved? And wow, look at the flex of his bicep.

"Want some wine or something?" he asked.

Wine? Have a drink, alone, with Justin Walker? Hadn't that been her dream for years?

Silly girl. She'd been alone with him for the last few weeks. The reason why cast a shadow over the thrill of his offer. "Wine sounds great."

"I promise the glasses are clean. Unless you want a beer."

"Wine to celebrate a successful tuck-in sounds better."

There was that grin again. The man had charm a county wide.

He went into the kitchen. She adjusted the collar of her sweater and let out a frustrated huff. It didn't matter what she looked like. Her outfit wasn't any different than it ever was. Cable-knit sweaters, leggings, and big fluffy socks. Some nights, she felt glammed up next to Justin, but she'd never complain. Those pajama pants of his rode low on his hips.

He entered, two full wine glasses sloshing in his hands. "I feel like there's a hint of my old self coming back. But I don't think I've ever drunk wine in pj's before."

"Boots and blue jeans instead?"

"Not quite." He took a long sip and closed his eyes. Long, dusty-blond lashes feathered across his cheeks. "Ah. Now that's the stuff."

She tasted it, putting the glass to her lips. Sweet liquid flowed over her tongue. Smooth. Rich. This *was* good stuff. Like what she'd find in Mom's wine fridge. "It's really quite good."

He'd laid his head back and shut his eyes, holding his wine on the armrest. He cracked an eye open. "Surprised?"

"Um…"

He chuckled. "Once upon a time, Priya." Blowing out a gusty breath, he closed his eyes again. "I wasn't always this guy."

"What did you used to do? Maisy only said you were some big shot."

"Big shot?" His laugh was full of derision. "I could've been, but my partner used me up and spit me out." He winced, like he hadn't meant to say that much.

Was that his type? Manipulators? Justin seemed like a confident guy with no interest in games. What did she really know about him? She wanted to know a lot more than she did. "And then you came back to Moore?"

"Yep." He sat up and took another drink, sucking his lips against his teeth. "Then I called Maisy. Look at me now." He hid the bitterness well. Did his family know any of this? "You know how you can't live without someone and you promise them the world—until they close a deal worth millions and all of a sudden, you need to move on? That was Gabrielle Hayes. It was supposed to be *our* company, but she maneuvered me out. She was a shark in the boardroom; I don't know why I didn't think she'd be the same way in her personal life."

Or he didn't think she'd be that way with *him*? "You trusted the person you loved. It shouldn't be a defect."

He set his wine down. "I don't have to worry about any of that anymore." Sprawling in the chair, he let his arms hang over the sides. "Never again. I'm done with relationships. And women altogether."

She averted her gaze from the way his long form stretched out in front of her. Done with women, huh?

Yet *she* was a woman. Here, helping him. His sister was

helping him. Were women only bad when he wasn't the one in control?

She should run long and far from a guy like him. Wasn't that what Emmett had been like? It was okay for her to sacrifice for his career, but he couldn't be bothered with her needs. The night she'd lost her first baby, she'd worked all night with the doctor she was training under. The mom had labored for hours, then they'd done a C-section—and lost the baby. In her mentor's words, "We saved the mother, concentrate on that." She'd held it together until she got home and collapsed on Emmett's shoulders.

And he'd held her. For a moment. Then he'd gently tucked her into the couch so he could go get a good night's rest for the liver transplant he was a part of the next day. Logical. No patient should have to suffer for her breakdown. Then logical became routine, until Emmett acted like her career was inconsequential next to his. Like babies practically birthed themselves and if women had gynecological troubles, Priya could just do a hysterectomy and voilá. Problem solved.

And Dr. Bezos wondered why so many patients had sought her out when she'd started. She suspected he shared Emmett's thoughts on women's health.

But transplant medicine? To Emmett, he was God's personal assistant, resurrecting people and giving them new life. And it still bothered her how much of a hole he'd left in her life when he'd moved away and told her she shouldn't come with.

Some nights she dreamed of the chance to show him how she'd moved on, and especially how she wasn't hung up on a man and catering to his every need. She snuck a glance at the rugged rancher sipping his wine in pj's. At this point, she might have to pretend.

CHAPTER 6

Another two weeks went by. Isaiah was sleeping longer and his colicky times were shorter. Justin sorted through bottles. Wide neck, narrow neck, bag bottles, angled bottles, and nipples of every shape and size. None of them worked miracles, but he cleared out the ones that definitely made Isaiah gassier than others.

The new routine his son had formed was almost doable. Once the colic went away, he might actually have consistent hours, with only one or two feedings at night.

The drawback was that Priya might not stop by anymore. He doubted she'd abandon him entirely, but their nightly chats were one of his favorite parts of the day. She didn't pressure him for details about his past, which made him weirdly want to talk about it more. He was proud of what he'd done. All the places he'd traveled had been perfect for a young guy trying to prove himself and live life to the fullest. The company... It'd had potential. But it had never been what he truly wanted to do. Gabrielle had been so utterly convincing.

You do the negotiating, I'll run the numbers. We make a good team. You know we do, baby.

How many times had she said, *We'll just land one more account? Stay on just a little longer. Look how far you've come.*

Now he was thirty and homebound. Exactly where he wanted to be. When Isaiah was older, they could travel. Justin had a nice chunk of savings built up, and soon he might even venture to the bank and open an account for Isaiah. Do the responsible thing and get the will and trust lined up.

His ears pricked up at the drone of a familiar engine. Priya was arriving. She spent all her free time helping him after long hours at the clinic. What did her parents think?

They have their own life. The tightness in her expression gave him the impression that when her parents' nest had emptied, they'd built their own life, and Priya moving back hadn't changed anything.

His phone rang just as Priya parked. His heart slammed at the number on his screen. He'd never called Maisy's parents and they'd never called him, but their number was plugged into his phone, just in case. He should've called.

Her mom was calling now.

"Hi, Katherine. How are you doing?"

"Justin." The wistfulness in her voice ate at him. Like calling him was a giant obstacle she was still trying to overcome and failing. "We're good. You know, as we can be. How are you? How's… Isaiah?"

Truthfully, he was surprised they hadn't called before. When the funeral had ended and he and Isaiah had been left alone, he'd thought he'd see them at the hospital. Then Isaiah had been discharged and Justin had gotten busy with him and he hadn't contacted them. With the colic, he hadn't given them more thought beyond wondering if they were going to be a part of his son's life.

He reclined against the back of the chair and prattled on about Isaiah and the last couple of months.

Priya entered on a swirl of cold air. She smiled at him and yanked off her stocking hat. Her hair was coiled into a bun-braid or whatever they were called. Her jacket's collar was as high as it could go, and she wore stylish winter boots with rubber soles. She was the sexiest snow bunny he'd seen in a long time, and his years in Denver gave him a lot of memories for comparison.

But Priya had always outshone the others around her. She had a natural radiance, she exuded sharp intelligence, and she was quiet—until you got to know her.

Why wasn't Priya the one he'd made a play for all those years ago?

She'd never thrown herself at him like Maisy had. No coy looks, no flirtatious giggles. As a boy with raging hormones and unwilling to experience rejection, he'd gone for the sure thing. Maisy had made it clear she was guaranteed.

Besides. He'd sworn off women. And if he hadn't, Priya wouldn't be the one he went after.

A sour taste lingered in his mouth. No, he wasn't going to be going after anyone. That declaration didn't feel right either, but it wouldn't be Priya. She was…just a friend.

"So, that's about it," he continued, not knowing how Katherine was reacting to his verbal vomit of all things Isaiah. He was one of those parents now. If someone asked him about his kid, he trapped them in a corner until he was done talking about his pride and joy.

Priya grinned at the baby strapped to his chest and wandered into the kitchen. He had food in the crockpot. He hoped she helped herself—and that it tasted good. Today, with the extra freedom baby wearing had given him, he'd resolved to do better in the food department.

Didn't mean he could do more than dump a roast in a pot. And vegetables. He included those now. For her.

I just feel better eating a veggie-heavy diet, and it's what I'm used to. Keep your meat. I'll eat around it.

Still, he'd simmered the carrots and potatoes in vegetable broth.

"I was thinking…" Katherine's timid start put him on alert. She blew out a breath like she was frustrated with herself. "We'd like to see him. Spend some time with our grandson."

He quickly mulled it over. Too long of a pause and she might think he was resistant to the idea. He wasn't. "Would it best if we all hung out for a little, get you used to his wily baby ways? I admit, he and I haven't parted since he's been home from the hospital, so I might have a harder time than he does."

"And leaving him makes you uncomfortable." She wasn't upset. More matter-of-fact. "I'll be honest, Justin. You know Maisy was an only child. I haven't been around babies in thirty years. So, yes, why don't you two come over and we'll figure this out?"

Relief poured through him. "I really want him to have a good relationship with his grandparents, especially when he's lucky enough to have a set that lives in the same town."

"Oh, Justin." A breathy catch on the other end clued him into her tears. "I was worried—I know you and Maisy had your issues, and I don't pretend to understand them."

"We can talk about that, too," he said quietly. He was curious to know if they blamed him for things between him and their daughter.

"In time," she sighed. "In time. There's so much we're coming to terms with now, but we thought putting off getting to know Isaiah only hurts us all."

"Tell me when and we'll be over." He pushed off the chair

and headed for the kitchen. Priya hadn't reappeared, and he had to know what she was doing, what she thought of his attempt at more than heat-and-serve food.

"Next Saturday? We're out of town this weekend."

"We'll do morning. He's been officially setting a nap time in the afternoon."

"Thank you."

"Don't thank me. You're his grandma." And doing this alone sucked.

Only he hadn't totally been alone. Clicking the phone off, he stopped in the doorway, a smile tilting his lips.

"That bad?"

Priya jumped. Her guilty glance widened his grin. "No." She caught his expression. A smile tugged at her own lips. "Not if you're a fan of just meat-flavored everything."

A hoard of seasoning bottles was clustered next to the crockpot. He succumbed to watching as she added a dash or two here and sprinkled some there. Then she grabbed a spoon and tasted the broth. As her red lips closed around the utensil, he stared, his heart doing a slow slam against his ribs.

She was clinical about the whole process. Efficient. Critical. And he was as enthralled as if she were in a lacy negligee, dancing around and swiveling her hips.

Heat engulfed him with that image. Swamped him until his heart pounded. They were just friends.

Just friends.

Just. Friends.

"Can you save it, Doc?" He had to break the silence—and the power one little thought had over him.

"This, I can save." Another cryptic comment. It wasn't in what she said, but what she didn't say. Something was going on in her life and he had a no-access pass.

That bothered him.

After Maisy, she'd been as no-nonsense as she was about

the roast. She saw what needed to be done and did it. But with each passing day, she was dealing with something she couldn't fix. A professional like her? It must be eating at her.

He would know. He used to be the same way.

Until he'd moved home. He'd rather deal with the changing sheep market and finicky Mother Nature than play people games in the boardroom—and in the bedroom.

She started digging in his cupboards. "I'll just add some noodles, if you don't mind. It won't take long."

"Of course I don't mind." She ate what he made, and he rounded out his meals better. For her. "I'll go lay him down."

She arched a brow. "Is he going to stay asleep after being hugged against you?"

"Probably not. But as much as this baby-wearing thing is growing on me, I can't afford to have a parasite stuck to me day and night."

Her lips quirked. She put the lid back on the crockpot and turned it to high. "Parasite?"

"Like one of those fish that stay suctioned to the sides of fish tanks."

She laughed, throwing her head back, and he couldn't look away from her graceful neck. What would it be like to nuzzle her skin? To hear her breathy sighs, feel the way it'd make her writhe?

Just friends.

He spun around and nearly ran for the stairs. His commitment to abstinence was biting him in the ass. He was used to going without for weeks. Even months, as he'd waited for Gabrielle to prove she was serious about them. Those times she'd decided she needed space, then yeah, he'd gone out and found company for a night, or a weekend. When he'd traveled and was single, he'd sampled more than the food. He could control the wants of his body and his mind. He prided himself on it.

The one time he'd failed, he'd ended up with a baby.

As he carefully released Isaiah from the wrap, he recommitted to his no-women declaration. While he was chin-deep in diapers and nap times, his libido would have to stay on maternity leave.

~

CRADLING the phone against her shoulder, she gazed at the chart on the screen in front of her. She was tucked away in her office. The door was closed. Any crying wouldn't be witnessed.

What she was getting told on the phone only made it harder to steel herself against the flood of tears.

"It's up to you," Justin said. "I don't want to take advantage of you, but he's settled into a nice routine. Three nights of no-crying fits. Think we're in the clear?"

Until teething started, but she didn't want to scare the poor guy. He sounded so hopeful. "He's almost three months old. He might be growing out of it."

Those last three nights, she'd had wine with Justin in his living room. They'd discussed Maisy's parents. His mom and dad and siblings. She'd talked about her sister. They were experts at chatting for hours without really diving deep into themselves. They reminisced about high school. She still had never confessed her feelings for him. Sitting across from him while he lounged in yet another pair of pajama pants, with his hair adorably rumpled and his beard inspiring all kinds of questions about how it'd feel against her skin, she always played it cool.

And the man had the best stash of wine.

She took a swig of her cold tea just to forget how much she enjoyed their time together. "I'll have my phone on me if you need help."

"I appreciate it. If I can get a handle on the nights, then maybe I can figure out how to ranch as a single dad."

That'd be harder.

Before he disconnected, she blurted, "Tell me how tomorrow goes."

He was going to the Jorgensons'. She worried for him. For them. For Isaiah, who she hoped wouldn't be pulled into the middle of any drama. Justin would move on with his life, meet someone else, maybe settle down. Her chest tightened at the picture in her head of his idyllic future. A scruffy Justin with his arm around another petite blond like Maisy, his adorable son running around at their feet. She wanted him to have a big, happy family. Even if she wasn't a part of it.

And why would she be? Justin didn't need her anymore and he was calling to tell her so. And even if he did want her around—what kind of message would pursuing her deceased patient's ex send to her decreasing patient base? Not everyone knew she and Justin had gone to school together and had their own history.

"Will do." Was it selfish to hate that he was building a comfort zone and not seeking her out? Then they'd go back to being friends, but not the close type that hung out all evening.

She wanted him to call her because he wanted to be with her. But that wasn't what their relationship was about.

Slipping her phone back into her purse, she squeezed her eyes shut for a heartbeat. Her next appointment was in fifteen minutes and she couldn't run from the results in front of her.

She'd have to tell the patient that she was losing her pregnancy. The mom was new to her, and this wasn't the news Priya had wanted to start their relationship with. Nor was she looking forward to the talk about polycystic ovary syndrome, but she couldn't find that the woman had been treated for it. Yet the signs were there.

An alert popped up on her screen. The patient was here and ready.

Rubbing the bridge of her nose, she mulled over her recent conversation. How comforting would it be to go to his place tonight, pour the wine, and spill all the stresses of her workday? After the next hour, when she had to tell someone some of the worst news of her life, Priya could use a trusted confidant, a shoulder to sob on in private, HIPPA be damned.

Part of the allure of moving home to work was that her parents were here. They knew all about how hard this job could be, and she could turn to them during these early years when she was still developing her own coping skills with the tragedies she faced. If they were ever around.

But Mom and Dad had surprised themselves with a weeklong trip to Mexico and were leaving tonight. This trip was a prelude to the cruise they had planned in March. And who knew where else they were going for the holidays? One thing Priya had gleaned from her brief conversations with them was that, with their kids off on their own careers, they didn't do many holidays at home. And they didn't plan to start just because Priya lived in Moore. At least they were spending Thanksgiving together.

Because it was only her.

If Devya flew to the U.S., Mom and Dad would plan the biggest holiday bash Moore had seen—the perks of being a free spirit instead of dependable and predictable. People relied on Priya when they needed her, and when they didn't, they left.

Justin was no different than anyone else in her life.

CHAPTER 7

The house looked exactly the same as it had years ago, the last time he'd visited. He hadn't been to the Jorgensons' as an adult. Maisy had tried to get him here, one of her many attempts to cocoon him in her web. He'd purposely kept his distance while maintaining civility he hadn't felt.

But here he was now.

Their rambler was comfortable. Familiar, with its twenty-year-old furniture and off-white paint job. He should've come to visit before, during, or after the funeral. All the reasons he couldn't dimmed now that he was here.

Lunch was finished, thank God. The most awkward meal he'd eaten in years. Isaiah had fallen asleep on the way to town and he'd suggested they leave him be. Let Isaiah rest and he'd be more cheerful when it came to holding and playing with him.

He'd regretted his request when talk had turned to Maisy, him and Maisy, and the circumstances around Isaiah's birth. The discussion had been long overdue, and it had gone better than Justin imagined. He had a newfound respect for

Katherine and Martin, and how they'd tried to help their daughter.

The atmosphere was relaxed now as Katherine cradled Isaiah. Martin peered over at least every five seconds, his face vacillating between grief and delight.

"Maisy had colic," Katherine announced. She jerked her head up like she'd startled herself. She put a hand to her chest and chuckled. "My word, Marty. Do you remember how hard that was?"

Martin developed a faraway look. "We used to joke that colic was the reason we only had one."

Katherine's gaze watered, but she recovered. "Right. She was a handful from the very beginning." Pressing her lips together, she looked away.

"She sucked her thumb, too."

Justin could high-five Martin for steering them out of deep waters.

For the next few minutes, Katherine and Martin reminisced and compared notes with him. Thumb-sucker? Pacifier? Does Isaiah have one pupil bigger than the other? He'll grow out of it. Has he found his toes yet?

The lightness of the conversation and the way the two grandparents treasured Isaiah prompted his next question.

"Do you guys want to spend the afternoon with him?"

Katherine's mouth opened, but no words came out. Then wonder crossed her face. "Would you be okay with that?"

"His diaper bag is fully loaded." Justin had packed less on international trips. "If he naps again, just cuddle him the entire time. He won't complain."

"We...we really appreciate this, Justin." Martin's face was close to crumpling. They had been legitimately scared he wouldn't allow them around Isaiah. He should've called earlier.

"Isaiah needs his grandparents." *He* needed Isaiah's grandparents.

After running through all the instructions, not like they'd need much, he shrugged into his coat. This was really happening. He could do…whatever he wanted.

Giving Priya a pass on baby duty with him had made the last few days lonely. Boring. Sipping wine by himself in his living room was not the high point of his day. In fact, watching the nightly news with a full glass and no one to talk to was his new low.

Leaving the house without his kid was like an expedition into the Outback. Other than enduring Isaiah's well-baby visits, he'd hardly ventured out. Brigit grabbed his groceries and chatted for a few minutes, but she was doing so much on the ranch he couldn't ask any more of her.

Blowing out a breath and watching it puff in front of his face, he ambled to his pickup.

Freedom.

Now what?

It was close to evening. He could go out and have a real meal—one he didn't have to cook himself, with food that needed actual preparation.

He wasn't that hungry, and going out to eat by himself didn't hold the appeal he thought it would.

As he pulled away from the curb, the phone popped into his hand before he thought too hard. A block later, he pulled over and called Priya. He shouldn't be calling her for no reason, but he couldn't bring himself to hang up.

She answered with "Is everything all right?"

He couldn't help his grin. Was it due to her question or just hearing her voice again? When had he started craving the sound? Probably when she'd quit coming every day. "Guess who's a free man for a few hours?"

"Free?" Fabric rustled like she was switching ears. "Like, no baby? Are your parents in town?"

"Nope. He's with Katherine and Martin."

"It went well then? How are they?"

He didn't miss how earnest she sounded. "They don't blame you, Pri." How could they?

"Everyone else does," she muttered and rushed on. "So what are you going to do?"

He mulled over her words. Should he ask her about it? Who blamed her? Why would she think that? Maisy's death had even been in the newspaper. Justin's parents had saved a copy for Isaiah when he was older, to help him know there was nothing that could've been done.

She spoke again before he did, her tone teasing. "It's a Saturday night even. The options are wide-open." Metal clanged in the background. Was she cooking?

Lunch hadn't been that long ago, but the memory of the magic Priya had worked with his crockpot roast was emblazoned onto his taste buds. "I only have a couple of hours. I was thinking of grabbing a meal that doesn't come with heating instructions for a half a bag or a whole bag."

Her laughter tinkled over the line. He liked that, making her laugh. "Where are you going?"

"I dunno. What are you cooking?" Look at that. He was hungry after all.

A squeak resonated from her end. He'd caught her off guard. Good. He liked doing that, too. The flare of her eyes and the hitch in her voice when he said something funny or that she wasn't expecting. She was serious. The stable one. He couldn't help but unsettle her—only in a good way. He hoped.

"Justin Walker, are you inviting yourself over to eat my risotto?"

While it sounded good, he could eat all her risotto and be

left wanting. He dropped his voice, wondering why he was going all seductive over food. "Is that all you're making?"

More laughter. "I can throw some pork chops in."

"I never pegged you for a rebel."

"Well, Mom said love wasn't enough to make a butcher's daughter give up meat. She has a stash in the freezer for when Dad works an evening walk-in clinic shift."

"Will they be around?" He hardly knew her parents, but he felt like he did after Priya's stories. Stories that just happened to be from when they were kids, not recent events.

Her sigh was heavy. "They took a whirlwind vacation to Mexico."

They had her house to themselves? That... He swallowed past his thick throat at the gathering of desire the information started in him. He shifted in his seat like the temperature had spiked from the mid-forties to triple digits. He tried to use humor to diffuse the tension coiling in his gut. "I'll invite my closest twenty friends. We'll have a rager like in high school."

"Don't you dare. Besides, they'd probably get overly excited and think Devya was home."

He blinked at the unexpected bitterness from her. Or was that jealousy? Combined with her cryptic comment earlier, he wanted nothing more than to corner her and talk.

Maybe not *nothing* more. His mind conjured so many things for the two of them to do alone. But no. This was just talking. She was a friend. She'd never indicated she wanted more.

"Just me and you." He enjoyed the sound of that too much. "No need to get anyone in trouble."

"Do you know where I live?"

It was Moore. Of course he knew where she lived. "Yeah, you're in Lakewood. The big house."

All the houses in Lakewood bordered on mansions. She giggled and gave him directions anyway.

He couldn't recall her house. Hadn't he ever been there? Thinking back, no, and as an adult he knew why. Maisy wouldn't have allowed him to go to another girl's house—with her or not, and especially not Priya's. The daughter of a doctor and nurse, and not just any doctor or nurse. The Patels were well-off. Grandfather Patel had been a doctor, and Priya's other grandparents owned a successful business. Her parents hadn't been stupid with money either. Justin doubted either of them had graduated with a penny in student loans.

Lakewood was the high class of their little town. He'd hardly driven through it, except maybe with his parents to look at Christmas lights.

The trip was short, but he slowed down in Lakewood. Around him, the homes reminded him of Denver, those mountain "lodges" that were really luxurious living. Priya's house rivaled their size and except for being noticeably older, it was as opulent. Stone veneer, dual-level porch, and he'd bet there was a Juliet deck in the back. The place was right off the water. Did they have their own dock?

Did Priya swim in the summer? Lay out in the sun, wearing nothing but a cherry red—

Where the fuck had his mind gone?

Just friends.

He parked behind the closest garage door to the house, next to her car. Wasn't there room in this monolith for her ride?

Sliding out, he studied the yard. Mature cottonwoods and evergreens lined the property. The landscaping was mostly dormant for the winter but still obviously professionally maintained. In June, this lawn was probably lusher than carpet.

He knocked on the door.

Her "come in" resonated from deep within the structure. Stepping inside, he closed the door behind him and stared.

He was in a foyer as large as his bedroom, and the arched ceiling soared over his head. A small window let in sunlight during the day and he could see all the way to the back of the house, where wall-to-wall windows framed a lake view.

"You don't want to walk naked through here, do you?" He toed off his boots.

"Unless someone's in the yard, you should be able to. The backyard is pretty private." Priya appeared to his right on the other side of an expansive dining room. She wore leggings, the black ones with sparkles. One of his favorite pairs. Her oversized sweater swallowed her whole—like he wanted to.

Heat licked up the back of his spine. Maybe coming here wasn't the best idea, but he couldn't bring himself to regret it.

THAT LOOK. Priya backed up a step. A giant of a woodsman stepped into her house, all rumpled and sexy in his jeans and flannel shirt. The intensity of his look pinned her in place. She was a rabbit caught in his crosshairs—and she didn't want out of them.

"Do it often?" he asked, his voice lowering to an octave that vibrated deep inside of her.

She held back a shiver. "Do what?"

"Strut through here naked?"

Her laugh came out far too nervous. "If it were my private house, maybe. But not when I'm living with my parents."

Just like that, the vacuum his presence had created flooded with air. He stood straighter, like he'd been ready to pounce but decided she was too scrawny for good prey.

The timer on the oven beeped as it reached its

programmed temperature. It was hot enough, and it wasn't the only one.

"Dinner isn't quite ready." The meat had yet to go into the oven. She spun and called over her shoulder, "The risotto should be done with the pork chops."

The wave of heat following her must mean that he was right behind her.

"Smells good." He was close. She didn't turn to look. It was hard enough to concentrate as it was. "But maybe a little burnt?"

This time she did turn and look at him over her shoulder. Burnt?

His blue eyes twinkled. "Just teasing."

"Ha. No pressure." She went through the motions of finishing supper, but her mind was on the man in the kitchen. "You could've gotten a professional meal. Instead, I have to represent."

"This'll be even better. Because you made it for me." They stared at each other for a heartbeat. "And it's free."

Perhaps the simmering tension between them had been her imagination. Wishful thinking. "I can do free."

"All kidding aside, Priya. This means a lot. Everything you do for me means a lot."

She removed the pot of risotto from the stove and flipped the burner off. She kept her back to him. "Of course." That was her. Reliable.

He planted himself against the counter next to her. "Hey."

He didn't say more but the burn of his gaze blazed into her. She peeled her gaze off the marbled granite and met his.

"What's wrong?" he asked.

She shrugged as casually as she could manage, but after the last three months, it was a piss-poor effort. "Nothing."

He tilted his head. "Really? I'm pretty dense, but I've picked up on some signs. Spill it."

Where did she begin?

Her family took her for granted, and while they were off having the time of their lives, they were all okay leaving her behind.

Or how about that all her friends lived in other towns and were also friends with her ex, who was off doing fabulous things? Meanwhile, she'd managed to lose the trust of all her patients, who were slowly and painfully canceling all their appointments and going to different doctors.

So, yeah, she might lose her job. Wouldn't that suck? To get fired in her own hometown? Who would hire her if the place she was *born* in wouldn't even keep her?

Even worse, they were leaving her because of what had happened to Maisy.

"It's just work pressure," she finally said.

He lifted a blond brow and slid closer. "I don't think so. You can talk to me, you know. We've done a lot of talking."

Her traitorous body turned closer to him as he faced her. "Because we're friends." Bravo. She kept the bitterness out of her voice.

"Friends…talk."

Her gaze dipped to his mouth. His whiskers weren't long enough to hide his lips. Would they tickle if she kissed him? "What else do friends do?"

The question evaporated between them, leaving no time for her to be mortified about what she'd said or how he'd interpret it.

"I hope they kiss, because I've been dying to do that for a while."

Her lips parted. His confession obliterated her good sense, and hope exploded like fireworks. He dropped his head and she stretched up to meet him.

Slowly, he pressed his mouth to hers. They were each tense, only their lips touching. Then he groaned, and she clutched his shirt. He wrapped his strong arms around her. To her, he'd always been taller, broader, just big. But as he swamped her, she gladly burrowed into him. His warmth, his strength, his solidness. It was all there for her.

He deepened the kiss, teasing her lips apart with his tongue. She reveled in the soft scratch of his beard and his faintly minty flavor. Letting go of his shirt, she took her time brushing her hands up his hard chest and around his neck.

He didn't stop. She was making out with Justin Walker in her house. Her teenage self would've never believed it.

Stooping, he gripped her ass, lifted, and turned. Her butt hit the counter and she automatically wrapped her legs around his waist. There was no moment of indecision, no wondering if she was doing the right thing or not. They were each succumbing to this...whatever...between them. She thought it'd been only one-sided, but he must've felt it, too.

He tipped his head and she met each stroke of his tongue with her own. She clamped her legs tighter, seeking some sort of release for the ache between her legs. He was the remedy.

She had no clue how much time went by. Lost in him, the world faded away. Chalk it up to not having been thoroughly kissed like this in a couple of years, or the mountain of man in front of her, but she was nowhere near done with him. She liked the gentle tickle of his whiskers, the way his hot breath wafted over her cheek as they synchronized their inhales and exhales, and the subtle rocking of his hips, as if the pressure building inside of him was as strong as hers.

Neither one of them seemed to be in any hurry to move further, as if it would shatter the bubble of intimacy around them and allow reality to crash in.

The alarm on the oven blared. She jerked, then instantly regretted her reaction. Would he think she was sitting here with her legs twined around him, ruing what they'd done?

The oven beeped again. The pork chops were thin, but had they made out for fifteen minutes? It had felt like ten seconds.

He stepped back, sucking in his lower lip and then releasing it slowly as his gaze swept her face.

The alarm continued to beep but she didn't move, and Justin didn't break out of the ring of her legs.

"That was unexpected," he said.

"Yes." She regarded him cautiously. Was he plagued with a case of the *we shouldn't haves*?

He swallowed, his Adam's apple working up and down. Her fingers twitched to stroke the area. Fine whiskers feathered down his neck. Were they as delightful to the senses as the ones on his face?

The *beep beep* of the alarm was as loud as a bullhorn. She released her legs and he stepped back. To her surprise, he held out a hand to help her slide down to the floor.

She hit the button to stop the timer and grabbed the oven mitts. Each second that ticked by, the air grew heavier. Were regrets weighing it down? How would she react if he got weird?

Was *she* going to get weird? There was a lot of history between them, but none of it sexual.

She plopped the pan of pork chops on the counter next to the cooling risotto and steeled herself. She faced him.

His arms were crossed and he was eyeing her from under hooded lids. The guarded expression he wore didn't clarify at all where he stood with what had just happened.

"Hungry?" She had no idea what else to say. The last guy she'd made out with had left her for his career, but he'd stepped out on her long before that. The breakup had been an   it's-not—you-it's-me-because-I-don't-want-to-be-tied-to-just-you thing. Not that it still stung or anything.

His look morphed from evaluating to sizzling hot like the pan behind her. He was hungry, but not for food.

She held her breath, refusing to be the first to act on it.

All at once, the tension drained out of him and he dragged in an audible breath. Tipping his head back, he stared at the ceiling. "We're friends, Priya. I don't want to risk that."

Someone might as well have tossed her in a snowbank. She wasn't enough for him to put in the effort.

"Me, neither." She hugged her arms around herself. Friend zoned. Justin had had a moment of weakness and she'd happened to be in the proximity. And she thought Emmett's breakup excuse had been humiliating.

"I'm sorry, I don't know what came—"

"Don't you dare." Her burst of anger was out of character, but her week had been too crappy to restrain it. "I've never been the sexpot who made men lose their minds, so if you keep going, it's going to sound like you're horrified you kissed someone like me."

His look of shock melted into amusement. "Every time you wear leggings you're a sexpot."

A hot flush smeared her cheeks. She always wore leggings. "Wait until you see me in scrub pants."

He flinched. "I have before. Once."

She was about to ask when, but then horror flooded her. The night Maisy had died. And here she was kissing him. "Oh. I'm sorry."

He shook his head. "Don't be. Not about—" His scowl danced around the kitchen before returning to her. "You and I are good. I don't hold anything that happened against you."

One of Maisy's office visits ran through her head. *Will a test tell me I'm pregnant this early?*

But you used protection, right?

Maisy's laugh still haunted her. She'd looked so hopeful. *It was so old, Pri. It totally broke. I had a new pack, but I saw that one lying in the drawer and figured it was destiny. Justin had come back to me after all.*

Since she was Maisy's doctor and had never written her a prescription for birth control, Priya had ordered the pregnancy test. Never had she wanted to break the rules more than when the result pinged on her computer. Positive, and she hadn't been allowed to give Justin a heads-up.

"She knew how to play both of us," she said.

"Yeah. Sometimes I suspect she did more than that." The intensity of his gaze deepened, like he was mentally ripping up the HIPPA policy and willing her to spill Maisy's office confession. When she didn't offer any confirmation, he propped one hand on the counter beside her. His other hand was on his hip, and he towered over her, but she didn't feel intimidated. More like protected. "No one but you understands how it was for me. No one but me understands how it was for you."

"And no one's going to know because you have a son to raise and he can't grow up hearing about how troubled his mom was."

"Yeah," he said softly. "If it helps, I know what came over me."

"Oh?" The heaviness drained out of the air around them.

"Yep. But I don't know if I should tell you." His expression turned cocky. "I don't know how you feel about me."

No way was she going to confess how she'd wanted him since puberty. But dropping the conversation now was just unfair. Couldn't she have, if not one night with him, at least one conversation? A few moments to pretend their past wasn't an emotionally loaded cannon with a short fuse? "You're a good-looking guy. And you happen to be a decent man."

"Just what every man wants to hear. I can hear the women falling over themselves now."

She giggled. "Stop it."

His expression sobered. "I trust you, and I can only say that about a few people. No one I've dated. I worry if we— I'm a single dad and I don't even know yet how I'm going to work and raise my kid at the same time. I need your friendship more than I need…you know."

"Sex?" The flare of heat in his eyes could've cooked the pork chops well done. "I'm a doctor, Justin. You can say it around me."

"If I say it, then I'll want it."

That shut her up. But not for long. No matter how he'd couched it, he didn't want to sleep with her. Or he didn't want to *want* to sleep with her. "Right. And we can't, apparently."

She stepped out from the cove he'd made around her. He was also blocking the food, but she could set the table. Time to prepare for the most awkward meal ever.

"Priya."

She opened the cupboard and yanked two plates out with more force than intended. Where did Mom keep the paper plates? Now she'd be stuck doing dishes with nothing to think about but Justin's rebuke.

"No, I get it." She rushed out to the dining room. "We're friends and you don't think we can be any more and not ruin our friendship."

True or not, after that kiss, she was willing to try. And wasn't that what bothered her? Her ass on the counter, grinding into him, was enough to make her toss their history and her career just to see how hot they could blaze into the future. But he was like, whoa, you're a better *friend*?

It chafed.

Because he was right. They understood each other as far

as Maisy's influence was concerned. Her patients didn't. They were already leaving. If anyone learned she and Justin were in a romantic relationship, the accusations would fly, and it was her career they would damage.

He followed her. She almost jumped at how close he sounded. "Do you really think we can sleep together and keep it casual?"

Her? No.

The fear of losing her job had just run through her mind, but here she was spinning out over "sleep together." And the key word: casual.

She wanted this. No one had to know. Her private life was just that.

She squared her shoulders and faced him. His challenging look propelled her to an answer she wasn't ready for.

"Yeah, actually. I think we can."

CHAPTER 8

His erection was finally starting to fade and then she hit him with that.

She wanted casual sex. With him.

The woman with the killer legs and the teasing tongue and the little whimpers when he ground against her wanted to sleep with him.

Oh, but Priya. I don't want sex. I don't want to sleep together. I want to fuck you until you agree this is the worst idea in history.

The problem was that it'd be too late. He'd get hurt. He'd want too much or not enough and she'd get hurt. Or worse, she'd lie to him. Use him. Manipulate him.

There it was. The real reason he had a hard time pushing farther than a spontaneous kiss.

"Maybe you can, but I've been used for sex before," he said. "And I've had sex used against me to trap me into more."

She deflated before his eyes, the defiant light in her eyes fading. "I guess I've been in the middle. No one cared enough either way."

He used to pride himself on how well he read people in the boardroom. But the last few years, he'd been around sheep and cattle or stuck in a combine or grain truck by himself. His skills were dull.

She thought she wasn't appealing enough for a guy to toss his doubts aside and jump in the sack with her.

He walked up to her. Her gaze remained fixed to his chest where she'd fisted his shirt. He tilted her head back.

"It isn't a bad thing to not be lumped into those categories."

"You mean not to be so dead sexy a guy would go stupid just to be with you? Or not to be so dead sexy a guy wouldn't even think about the complications sleeping with you would cause?" Her lips thinned, but they were still unfortunately lush. "I'm in the middle. So perfectly…dull."

How could she think she was dull? Her beauty was like the first spring ride on horseback after a long, bitter winter. And her brains? Looks were one thing, but someone he could spend hours talking to was a person he wanted to keep around. But he knew what she meant. Didn't mean he agreed.

He couldn't help himself. Touching his lips to hers, he kept it only a peck. "It's okay to be the one guys respect."

"Right. It's a well-known fact that all guys list 'respect' as the number one thing they want in a partner."

Her flat tone made him chuckle. "It's like one of those things that's a given and doesn't need to be mentioned."

She waved him off. "Regardless. I hadn't planned on discussing my lack of a love life—or any social life whatso-ever—tonight. I'm not looking for pity, or a pity lay. Let's consider the topic dropped and move on." She charged toward the kitchen.

Damn this big-ass house and her speed. He used all his height to catch up with her. This topic was not dropped, and he couldn't let it go. "Now, you can't hang casual sex in front of me and then drop it." He should let it stay dropped and forget it.

He should not be feeling this way about his ex's friend and doctor. Maisy's death should be a burden on their relationship, not something that brought them closer.

"I didn't drop it," she said. "You did." That's right. He'd tried.

"Because it was the honorable thing to do." He was tired of being honorable. Not the kind that would use Priya and discard her. There had to be a middle ground. The more distanced they got from that blistering kiss in the kitchen, the more he regretted his instant dismissal that it wouldn't work.

"Justin. I get it. As your friend, I'm not going to pressure you into anything between us that's out of your comfort zone."

He advanced on her. She backed her tight little ass up to the counter, but she didn't sidle around him and dart away. "You get that I wouldn't be in this for a long-term relationship. You get that it would just be a release for both of us. And that we'd use all the protection possible to prevent any and all chances of a pregnancy."

Her expression darkened. "I'm not the type to trap you into anything."

"I know you're not the opportunist Maisy was."

Her mouth tightened. "Right."

Did she also suspect Maisy had lied about protection? His first mistake was not using the condom he'd had in his wallet, but the one Maisy produced had looked good enough…in a dark room, when he was in a rush to forget everything.

Did Priya know something, and if she did, would she say anything?

No. No one could take back the result, and he'd never

give up his son. That part of his past would stay there. It couldn't come back and hurt him again.

"We can be reasonable adults. Just sex between friends." When he'd woken up this morning, he wouldn't have believed he'd be having this conversation before dinner—much less with Priya.

"Between *us*. Exclusive friends with benefits."

He blinked. That sounded a lot like a relationship. He had no plans to sleep with anyone else, no interest either, but her request was a little too earnest.

She rubbed her hands over her face. "Oh God. What am I doing? Never mind."

"No." He inched closer until he towered over her. "Exclusive friends with benefits. Agreed."

Her throat worked as she swallowed, and he couldn't look away. It gave him dirty thoughts that were suddenly attainable and not a thought he had to kick out of his head. Like he'd been doing since she first arrived to save his ass.

"So..." Her gaze darted around. If it weren't for her nerves the air would sizzle between them. He held his position to keep from scaring her away. "When do we start?"

Now. Fuck, he could do it now. Right here.

His intelligent brain kicked in. He had zero condoms on him. After he'd learned he was going to be a dad, he'd tossed them all. Without any, he wouldn't go roping his life to another woman. Was Priya on the pill? One of those ring things? Or that thing that gets stuck up there inside them? All three? Maybe she had condoms.

No. He wasn't trusting that decision to anyone else again.

Priya was waiting for him to answer, uncertainty creeping into her gaze.

"You and the baby dictate the schedule." He shrugged, like planning sex was the most mundane thing he'd ever done. "I don't think I'll have to sneak women around until he's a toddler. A boy with no mom doesn't need a stream of women coming and going."

Did he imagine the flash of hurt in her eyes? He had to be honest about what his life allowed.

"I can come over—" Her gaze unfocused like she was running her schedule through her pretty little head.

"Tonight." He loved the way her delicately arched brow peaked higher. By now, he knew her schedule. She wasn't on call.

"Tonight?"

"I have to pick up Isaiah after we eat. That'll give us time to think." Though he didn't want to wait. If that kiss was any indication of what being with her would be like, he'd drive himself crazy playing the waiting game.

She stared at him while his heart hammered with each tick of the clock. "Tonight, then. Our food is probably cold."

"Worth it."

She sputtered a laugh. "I'll finish setting the table and you grab the meal."

Eating with her after agreeing to sex in a few hours was a slow form of torture. He spent half the meal watching her lips close around her fork. The delicate way she chewed. How she tilted her head and studied her plate as she swallowed, like she was strategizing just how to scoop up her next bite. She stuck to her risotto and he cleaned up the two pork chops.

"I have cupcakes for dessert," she said as they each finished the last of their meal. "Homemade."

His stomach instantly made room. Anything this woman made, he'd eat. His taste buds seemed to form a special attachment to any food prepared by her.

"You bake, too?" They'd spent so much time together recently, he felt like he should know that. Yet she'd never brought over goodies, homemade or otherwise.

"I bake when I'm... To relax. I needed a little extra kick after this week." She got up and disappeared into the kitchen. He cursed the long sweater for hiding the sway of her ass.

When she reappeared she held a round stand with a wide base in her hand. A dozen cupcakes with delicate pink and green frosting were stacked on top.

"Are those flowers?" A smile lifted his lips as he imagined Priya concentrating over a piping bag. That little line forming between her brows, her lips puckered in concentration.

"A poor version, yes. I haven't had much time to play in the kitchen since I started working." She scooted the serving dish closer to him and took a seat. "Until now." That cryptic tone again.

He snagged a sweet. "Why now?"

She stilled for only a moment while peeling away the wrapper. "I'm home," she said lightly. "Back to cleaning ladies and yard service."

Justin looked around. "No shit? They hire out all that?" He could hire someone to cook, but with a big family, he didn't need more people in his business.

"Mom and Dad want to be free to do what's important. When we were kids, the stress was on studying, not vacuuming—more so for me, at least—and experiencing the world outside of Moore, though I wasn't encouraged to travel as much as Devya." Another shadow crossed her face. Did she miss traveling? "You may have noticed I liked to tidy things."

"Oh yeah. I've noticed." The corner of the nursery was back to its disaster zone state since she hadn't been there, and a pile of dishes waited to get loaded in the dishwasher.

"It's a good outlet for me when life gets overwhelming. But here..." She waved her arm around and rolled her eyes.

"Constantly clean."

"Exactly."

"I'm sure your parents would rather you concentrate on other things than cleaning their house."

"Their days being tied down are over. They've moved on to travel." Her tone was flat as she nibbled the icing off her dessert.

Okay. She wasn't going to be more forthcoming. Then all he could do was to take her mind off whatever bothered her. To do that, he'd have to keep the night moving.

While she picked at her cupcake, he polished off two more using less than stellar table manners, then cleaned up the dishes. She may like cleaning, but he had other plans for her energy. It was time to go.

"I'll text you when I get home," he said.

She followed him to the door. The house really was nice. The mix of upscale Midwest with sudden bursts of color was so...Priya. Nothing like his old ranch house, which had survived two boys and a tomboy sister.

He turned to face her. She hugged her arms around herself. Back to being self-conscious. It was cute, but he wanted to reassure her. "No pressure. Seriously. We're only going to do what you're comfortable with."

"Rule number one about exclusive friends with benefits?"

"That's not talking about it, which I didn't plan to do." He stepped into his boots and nodded his head toward her before he slipped out the door.

The cool air wafted over and around him. Just what he needed. Thankful to avoid the awkwardness of buying protection while carting a baby around, he made a quick stop at the gas station, then navigated the short drive to the Jorgensons'.

He sat in his truck for longer than he meant to. Why was guilt creeping in for picking up his kid? Maybe it was the box of condoms on the passenger seat. His ex's parents had watched his son while he'd made plans for sex with their late daughter's best friend.

What a fucking mess. But they didn't have to know. No one would find out. He got out and jogged up the walk. Martin met him at the door.

"Katherine's getting him buckled in." Martin beamed and gestured for him to enter. "We really had a good time. Thank you."

"We'll make this a regular occurrence. I think we all need it."

Martin ducked his head. "So, what'd you do with all your free time?"

Justin saw no reason to lie. The truth was a small outlet for his guilt. "I met Priya for an early dinner. She was a huge help during those long nights."

A serious expression descended over Martin's face. "Yes. Priya." Martin dropped his voice. "She's another one on our list. I worry that…that she thinks we blame her like the rest of the town."

"The rest of the town?" Hadn't Priya said something similar?

Martin peered around the corner of the entry where Katherine could be heard cooing to Isaiah. "Has she mentioned anything? I guess patients are dropping her as their doctor and she's in danger of losing her job." He let out an uncharacteristic snort. "People tell us this like we'd support the destruction of Priya's career." His voice lowered. "Katherine and I owe her a lot, and not just for saving Isaiah. She kept Maisy on the straightest path possible."

"She hasn't mentioned anything." Justin forced a smile. The bitter aftertaste in his mouth was too much like betrayal. Why wouldn't she talk to him? "But that'd be just like her, not wanting to worry me."

He said his goodbyes and drove home with his son. Isaiah

fell asleep once they hit the highway. The silence left him with his thoughts about Priya.

She hadn't confided in him. It was her life, her troubles. He had no right to them. But he'd asked. More than once. And she hadn't trusted him. So what did that say about their upcoming arrangement?

HER HANDS TREMBLED as she clenched the steering wheel. *I can't believe I'm going through with this.* She hadn't even showered, or primped, or changed clothes, and the debate about whether or not to do any of the above had driven her crazy. She'd opted not to. They'd made the deal while she was in her Saturday home-all-day clothes. Doing anything more would seem…needy? Presumptuous? Or worse, humiliating if he changed his mind.

She'd made this drive so many other times, but tonight was different. So, so different.

She still couldn't believe the conversation. Who talked about those kinds of things? Was that how it was done? She was in over her head. This wasn't her. This wasn't how she'd ever dated before.

But this wasn't dating, was it?

Exclusive friends with benefits. She'd ask herself what the hell was that anyway, but the description was right there. They would have sex, they would be friends, but they wouldn't plan a future together. Their lives would be otherwise separate. There was something so bittersweet about all of that.

Could she convince herself that this was casual? Could she keep her heart out of her head? Justin didn't know that she'd longed to be his for so many years. He didn't know that for the last month she'd wondered what it would be like if they were an item. A couple. Justin had the ability to make whomever he spoke to feel like the only other person in the room. She found it intoxicating.

She blamed all her exes, the few that she could count as an ex. None of the men she'd dated, especially not Emmett, had treated her like she was special. At first she'd thought Emmett might be the one, but she'd confused his treatment with his love for himself. She'd helped him succeed by pushing him through med school, and that was more important to him than anything. Professional stature meant more to him than any girlfriend ever would.

She swung into Justin's driveway and parked in her normal spot behind his garage door. The garage wasn't attached, and her spot was the closest to the house. He kept it clear for her.

Killing the engine, she let out a slow breath. Before she could lose her courage and put the key back in the ignition and floor it out of there, she climbed out of the car. The cold wind slapped her face, like it was asking what the hell she was thinking.

The house loomed over her. She tipped her head back to look past the roof to the black night sky above it. How many other times had she been here in the last several weeks? It felt like she was going into an alternate version of the house. It was a little darker, a little more warped than she recalled, as if she were looking at it through a carnival mirror.

Her footsteps crunched over the gravel. The stairs creaked ominously in the night. She did her usual tap on the door and stepped inside, but nothing about those actions felt normal anymore.

The place was quiet. Only a dim light in the living room was on. She glanced around but couldn't find Justin right away. Her taut shoulders eased.

Seriously. She'd had sex before, and she enjoyed it, as long as all body fluids were contained. Was that why planning to sleep with Justin was tumbling her insides like this? He'd want raunchy and she didn't do…messy.

No, she didn't want to get drizzled with chocolate for him to lick off. That was someone else's fantasy, someone who didn't let the threat of yeast infections turn them off. That extended to whipped cream and food play of any sort.

And no, she didn't find lube or semen on the couch cushions or carpet sexy. Maybe she should be so driven out of her head with passion it wouldn't matter. But it did, and guys seemed to be insulted by her restraint, and by how she liked to sleep in clean sheets and not ones that smelled like sex from two days ago.

She stepped out of her boots, shrugged off her jacket, and hung it up. Soft creaking from the stairs resonated through the silence. Tiptoeing into the living room, she almost bumped into him.

"I just laid Isaiah down," he said softly. "He fell asleep on the way home."

She nodded and stood awkwardly like she'd never been in the house before.

"Want some water? A glass of wine?" He was looking at her like she was a timid colt ready to bolt. Could he sense how poorly she was doing at being casual?

"Perhaps a small glass of wine." She wanted a clear head, but half a glass of pinot noir might dull the edge of her anxiety.

A slight smile played over his lips. "Make yourself comfortable. I'll be right out."

She flopped into the seat she usually took when they had their late-evening chats. She couldn't deny how right it felt to be back again.

Justin entered the room again, a glass in each hand. "Did I tell you that I'm actually going to try and get some work done tomorrow?" He handed her a glass with barely a tip of wine in it. His own didn't have much more. "Caleb and Brigit are coming over. We're going to do some work with the ewes." He dropped into his normal chair. He wasn't settled on the end, like he expected they would jump in the sack right away. More tension drained out of her body. "We hope that between the three of us, we can actually get out there and do some work with a baby in the house. You?"

"It's one of those days of total freedom I thought I wouldn't get many of when I first started my career." She dropped her gaze to inspect the rim of her glass. The topic of her abysmal career outlook was always on the tip of her tongue around him. She had no wish to go crying on his shoulder or anyone else's. Her life, her problems.

"How's work going?" The gravity in his voice lifted her gaze away from her wineglass. Had he heard something? Or was he that astute at reading her expressions? Likely both. They used to communicate by expression only around Maisy. "Martin mentioned something about Maisy's death being held against you."

All the tightness that had eased since she first entered the house flooded back until her shoulders ached. "Oh, that."

She didn't want to talk about work, but at the same time she *should* talk about work. She should talk to someone about what was going on, how she feared for the career she'd worked so hard for, and how to deal with the aftereffects of failing so spectacularly in front of everyone. All that on top of mourning her best friend, the one she'd worried about and pushed away at the same time.

"Do people really blame you?" he asked.

She went for honesty. Justin cared enough to ask, and she couldn't deny the warm feeling that gave her. "I think they do. I think they're scared. Even as a doctor it's hard to understand what happened, but I have years of training and access to other people's experiences with freak, traumatic situations. But even with all that, someone died. Not just anyone, but a young girl in her prime. I was in charge of her care. It's hard for others who don't understand the situation to see beyond that."

"I don't mean to sound callous, but people die all the time. Young people, old people, healthy people—even in Moore. But I don't hear of the other doctors having issues."

"I don't know if they realize how it's affecting me. They're…leaving for other doctors." She sucked her bottom lip in and released it slowly. "I admit, it doesn't make sense. It's like they hear things, they don't think too hard on it, but then when it comes to making an appointment, they choose a different doctor. Or they think of a reason why another doctor would be better for them. I don't know that they put Maisy's death together with why they don't trust me."

"Is there anything you can do?" Justin set his drink down and leaned toward her. The move was so supportive, the most support she'd gotten outside of Krista's pep talks.

"Keep being the best doctor I can with the patients I have." The few she had left, but she couldn't admit that. She didn't want to talk about it anymore. The humiliation she'd worried about was getting turned down for sex, not the shoddy state of her job. She latched on to a subject change, one she'd been wondering about for months. "How are Martin and Katherine really doing?"

"Good. Their healing is slow, but they're dealing with it." He chuckled. "I think they're going to spoil Isaiah silly."

"That's good."

Justin watched her for a moment, his eyes leveled on her. She gazed back, loving how the dull light made the gold flecks in his irises twinkle. It seemed a foolish thought in the moment to think about the color of his eyes. But they had enough gold to be classified as hazel. At first glance they looked like the bright blue of the Atlantic, or the blue of a rainbow. When she'd flown on vacations with her parents in high school, she used to look out the plane window at the expansive blue sky with the bright sun and think of Justin.

She couldn't escape the feeling that he saw under her facade. Maybe not far, but deep enough that he knew she wasn't being completely honest with him. She also couldn't escape the feeling that it bugged him. The same intuition had dogged her earlier when he'd been at her house. How could he know her well enough when her own parents were oblivious?

"Come here." The timbre of his voice wasn't one she'd heard from him before. It was lower, more…suggestive.

Her heart hammered hard enough to rattle her ribs. Like, *come here* come here? Were they starting? This was where she historically blew it. Her exes might not have complained about her performance, but more than one had commented on how getting her out of her own head was the real fore-play. She had a hard time shutting her mind off when it came to sex.

And again, as if he knew she was trapped in the hamster wheel of her thoughts. "Come. Here." Firm, but gentle.

He sat back, stretching his legs out in front of him. She rose and took the three tentative steps toward him. He held his hand out.

Her gaze stuck on that big hand. So strong, so capable. Hands that she never thought would touch her except for a friendly pat on the back, or a "Hey, how are you?" slug on the shoulder.

She reached out and connected with him, slipping her palm into his. Warm skin enveloped her hand, and his strong grip closed around her. She toppled into his lap, but he deftly caught her, draping her legs across his.

"How come you never told me about work before?"

"You have enough going on." And because she didn't want to seem needy around him. She wasn't the needy one, never had been. It wouldn't do any good. There was never anyone there who had her back.

"I thought you'd say that." He caressed her face with his other hand. She turned her head toward him until their lips were only inches apart. "Always taking care of others."

She prided herself on the way she took care of others, yet the way Justin said it was almost a criticism, like a word of caution. She took care of others to her own detriment, and he saw that.

His thumb stroked her lower lip. She instinctively leaned toward him. Their lips touched, and there was only a second, then two, before the kiss deepened.

Then they both exploded in hurried movements. She tugged his shirt up. He sat up to give her room to remove it while yanking hers up, too. There was no more talking, no more hesitation, no more soft touches. They both wanted sex, and they both wanted it now.

CHAPTER 9

$\mathcal{H}$e wanted sex and he wanted it now.

More precisely, he wanted it with her.

Sure, he'd anticipated sex before. There'd been times he was so worked up that he almost finished as soon as he dropped his zipper, but that hadn't happened for years. He'd had enough practice since then.

This could be one of those times, but he wanted to savor her. Desire banged around his brain. What if she decided this wasn't for her? What if she said nope and walked out? What if he really did finish before he'd properly tasted her, or seen her without a stitch of clothing, or felt how her body clenched around his when he brought her to orgasm?

Learning the answers to all that was critical, and he'd never experienced this level of urgency before. Definitely not the need to linger, to savor, to find out just how hard she could come.

Staying in this chair was a stupid idea. He couldn't spread her out like he wanted, but the light was on in this room. His bedroom would be dark. He wouldn't allow Priya to hide from him.

Then maybe she'd actually talk to him.

They were friends, dammit.

Except he didn't have any friends he wanted to fuck as badly he wanted to Priya.

His lips were on hers, but she'd stiffened again. That mind of hers was always going. His mission tonight was to be the center of her thoughts.

He finally wrestled her sweater off. She was gripping at his, but with the way she was twisted in his lap, she wasn't succeeding. He broke apart and reached behind him to rip the garment over his head.

Her hands were on him. Skimming over his shoulders, down his biceps, over his chest. Her eyes devoured him, and he needed the time. His own hungry gaze was busy. A black lacy bra cupped soft breasts with just a hint of nipple peeking through. It was the most erotic thing he'd ever seen.

Sliding his arms under her legs and back, he lifted her enough to scoot to the floor while folding his legs under him. She gasped and clung to him as he hit his knees.

"What are you—"

"I'm spreading you out." He set her on the carpet and rolled between her legs. The leggings were even better when he could view the full length of her curves. But they had to come off.

The frown on her face made him pause. She wiggled her butt, but not out of need. "Shouldn't we…lie on a blanket or something?"

"Do you think my carpet is that dirty?"

She slumped under him. "No, but what we're doing…" An adorable blush tinted her cheeks, but not from embarrassment. Frustration. At herself.

Did Priya's fastidious nature extend to the bedroom? The urge to find out consumed him. "Ever fucked on a floor before?" he drawled.

The blush deepened, but she scowled at him. "Y-yes."

Doing it on the bare floor bothered her enough to say something, but she was hesitant to talk about it. Someone had given her shit about her ways before. He didn't like that.

He settled on his forearms and let some of his weight rest on her. This time the hip wiggle wasn't from the wrong type of dirty thoughts. "Before or after you laid a blanket down? Or a towel?"

Her eyes narrowed, and she wasn't the pliant Priya she'd been on his lap. "I'm not going to answer."

"I told you, whatever you're comfortable with." He rose to his knees and flicked open the clasp of his jeans. Tonight would've been a good night to wear pajama pants. "You want a blanket, we're going to get a blanket."

The way she softened answered any of his questions about how guys had reacted in the past to his tidy doctor. Besides, they were friends, right? Then she should be comfortable with him.

He shoved the denim over his ass cheeks, yanking his underwear down with his pants. His shaft sprang free. Her lips parted when she looked at him. Yeah. A guy could get used to that reaction.

He dropped to one hand, hovering over her, and enjoyed how she automatically widened her legs to make room for him and draped her hands on his shoulders. But he didn't touch her.

Stretching, he snagged a throw from the couch. Sitting back on his knees, he liked the way she attempted to quit looking at his body and failed. Disappointment shadowed her eyes when the blanket covered his erection.

He fisted the material. "Lift your butt."

She sucked in the side of her lower lip. "You don't have to. We don't—"

"It makes you more comfortable."

"You don't take it as a personal affront to your masculinity that you can't bang the anxiety out of my mind?"

Who had said that to her? "I can't 'bang the anxiety' out of your mind if I'm stressing you out at the same time."

Her gaze softened, her concerns physically draining away. She leaned up to snap the blanket out of his hands. She shoved the material under her and helped straighten it out. Once she was settled, he cocked an eyebrow at her. Her answering smile was all the permission he needed.

"Those leggings. Off." He pointed at her. "You do it." He wasn't going to miss one second of finally getting to see her legs.

She worried her lower lip again, but hooked her fingers under the waistband. The little tease only peeled down her bottoms. Black, lacy underwear that matched her bra was even better dessert than her homemade vanilla bean cupcakes.

It wouldn't matter what type of undergarments Priya wore. She was as curvy as a centerfold and her skin glowed, but this set accentuated the flare of her hips and the round-ness of her bust.

"Underwear. Off." He was hard and throbbing, but he still hadn't moved. She was laid out before him and he had more to see.

She slipped her fingers under the thin strip of material that circled her waist, then hesitated. She was getting nervous again. Covering her hands with his, he pulled down, rolling the fabric with him.

Soft swells were bared, and fuck, the neatly manicured dark patch of hair was almost his undoing. He was going to bury himself there, but not yet.

Tossing her underwear aside, he settled back over her, keeping his hips angled up. He couldn't afford to lose his mind, and if his cock landed anywhere near her heat, he'd make bad decisions. But the funny thing was, he knew she'd stay levelheaded enough to make sure they were both protected.

He just didn't want to give her reason to worry and diminish her pleasure. He tugged down the lacy cups covering his personal paradise. Her breasts popped out. His mouth watered as he lowered his head to capture one between his lips.

Her soft exhale was followed by her arching into him, giving him the perfect opportunity to sneak his hands under her and unfasten the bra.

They were naked. "Now we can get started." He rocked up to land a hard kiss on her lips, then he nibbled and kissed his way down her neck, over and across to each nipple, then over the dip of her belly.

Finally, he was right where he wanted to be. Her hands tangled in his hair. A sudden mischievousness overtook him. This was the first time he'd had any sort of beard.

Hooking her leg with an arm, he grazed her inner thigh with his whiskers.

She bucked off the floor. "Justin!" She relaxed, but her legs were draped over his shoulders. Perfect. "You're naughty."

He chuckled as he settled onto his elbows. "I might be." Another light brush of his chin against her might send her off the blanket, but he caught her and made his move.

He nuzzled her, careful to minimize the effect of his beard, and licked through her crease until he hit her clit.

Her long moan echoed exactly what he was feeling. Finally. This was more amazing than he'd expected. And he couldn't wait for more.

She was wet, and as he licked and sucked on her tender flesh, she groaned, then caught herself. There was a baby sleeping in the house and neither one of them wanted to be interrupted.

She wriggled against him, getting close to her peak. Like with her undressing, he didn't want to miss a thing and he had a limited view where he was. A spectacular view. But he couldn't see the way her eyes sparked with passion, or how her breasts were thrust toward the ceiling when she bowed against the floor.

Her legs were tight around him, energy coiling in her body. Her gasps and pants were coming quicker. He made his move. Rubbing his thumb over her clit to replace his tongue, he used his shoulders to wedge her legs apart as he rose. At the same time, he slicked one finger inside of her.

Her mouth dropped open at the same time her legs went slack. This was it. She was going to come.

"I want to see it all, Pri. Come for me." He timed his strokes with the circles of his thumb.

She broke apart, and he got the only seat in the house. His Priya came undone as she moaned her release, his name on her lips.

He throbbed so hard it was uncomfortable. But worth it. So worth it as his little anxiety-ridden goddess orgasmed with nothing but his hand on her.

As she tumbled off her peak, her chest heaved, and she opened her eyes. The blush was back, but her look was unrepentant.

"You needed that," he said.

She only nodded, her gaze dreamy like she was still trying to come back down to earth. The fan of dark hair behind her head contrasted with the carpet. The flooring framed her body, and together with the saddle-brown throw, she was the most beautiful art in his house.

"You're going to get it again." That was big talk he wasn't sure he could back up. Eventually, he'd live up to his promise, but this first time would be kind of dicey. He reached for his pants and dug out the condom he'd tucked in a pocket earlier tonight. The rest of the box was in his bedroom, where he hoped they ended up after this.

He wasn't done playing with his exclusive friend with benefits.

The word *friend* left a drab stain on his mood, so he pushed the thought away. The benefits part was all he was busy with at the moment.

Rolling on the condom provided more stimulation than he wanted. He was afraid it'd take seconds off the final act, time he couldn't afford.

Pressing his palm against her center, he made tiny circles. She was wet and molten against him. Her prolonged moan was promising. Maybe he could help her come again.

She started squirming against him. "You're being an awful tease."

"Is this better?" He squared himself between her legs. They were nearly touching. He caught her gaze as he fisted himself and pushed against her entrance. The way her lips parted encouraged him.

He swung back and thrust forward, but only a little farther. She whimpered at the same time he groaned. She was liquid heat and so fucking tight. This time, he didn't pull out all the way, only enough to coat himself in her wetness and push back inside. A few times and he was fully seated inside of her.

His chest burned from holding back. Propping his arms on either side of her, he held himself high enough to watch as he impaled her soft folds. She was wrapped around him down to his base and her legs were twined around his hips.

She arched up to land a kiss at the base of his throat.

Another groan left him. "I'm not going to last long enough to make you come if you keep doing that."

"What?" she asked innocently. "This?"

Her teeth scraped along his skin and her blistering tongue

stroked over a nerve that sent shudders through his body. To top it off, she was rocking her hips as she adjusted to his size.

"Who's the fucking tease now?" he growled and dropped to one elbow. He wedged his other hand between them. All he had to do was rest a finger on her soaked clit. Their bodies did the rest.

She gasped his name, her breath feathering over the suddenly sensitive skin of his neck. As if she sensed what she was doing to him, she licked along his collar line. Her breathy moans and little whimpers caressed where her tongue had marked him. The sudden cooling of his heated skin pumped energy into his body.

His thrusts were harder, and his technique went out the fucking door. In and out, that was all he had a mind for. At least he managed to keep his hand between them.

Her body tightened around him at the same time she squeezed with her legs.

He might actually be able to do this. The base of his spine was already tingling, and his balls were hitched up as far as they could go. He was so close to climax.

Just a few more thrusts. The sounds of slick flesh slapping and their grunts and moans filled the room.

"Pri," he gasped into her ear. "You gotta come for me, baby. I can't wait."

Like his voice was the magical missing ingredient, a flood of heat coated him as she released. His orgasm slammed into him, flooding him with all kinds of euphoria he'd never experienced before. Was this the climax of a man who'd gone without for a year?

As he floated down from his high, Priya's arms stayed around him. His shoulders stung from where she'd scored him with her nails.

Alarm widened her eyes and she snatched her hands back. "I'm so sorry. Did I hurt you?"

He gave her a lazy smile while managing not to collapse on top of her. "Feel free to hurt me like that anytime."

She giggled and glanced away. When she looked back, she dropped her voice like she was telling him a secret. "I've never scratched anyone during sex before."

The male ego was a greedy thing. His bloomed so large he was surprised his head still fit in the room. "I never had a beard during sex before. It's a useful tool." He cocked his head to listen for any sounds of Isaiah awakening. Since getting over colic, he usually woke once at night for a bottle.

He heard nothing. A look at the clock told him it was early yet. He slipped out of Priya and loved how her delicate body shuddered as he did. She was still sensitized.

He leaned down and nipped her earlobe. She squeaked but clung to him harder as he whispered, "He's still asleep. Want to take this playdate to the bedroom?"

THE TANGLE of sheets around her legs was new. Priya scissored her legs and kicked them off. She scrunched her face without opening her eyes. What had awoken her?

A loud knock echoed through the house into the bedroom. Justin's bedroom. Where she was still naked and it was morning.

She sat up with a gasp. Since she'd kicked the blankets off, she had to scramble to find a sheet to pull over her torso.

"Justin," she hissed.

He was sprawled next to her. The man took up as much of the bed as possible. A guy used to sleeping alone. She wouldn't think about the satisfaction that gave her.

He wasn't wearing any clothes either. They'd had sex until only a few hours ago. The delicious stiffness in her muscles and the faint taste of condom on her tongue would attest to that.

Her first thought was…he'd promised to clean the sheets this morning. All because he knew it would be on her mind otherwise. She liked clean sheets and the doctor in her liked body fluids in their place. He had intuited not only her preferences, but that it had been a sore spot her previous boyfriends picked at. Now she wasn't as embarrassed about it as she used to be.

Her second thought was how magnificent he looked. Like…*damn*. She'd never been an admirer of genitalia. Privates were her job and in real life, on real people, they looked nothing like what Hollywood or any magazine portrayed. Penises were just not a mouthwatering body part.

Then there was Justin. His half-flaccid dick was draped across his thigh as he slumbered, and it was impressive. She knew the science behind morning wood, but it didn't diminish his appeal. Or the fact that she could stare at him all morning.

The knocking came again. Along with a female calling for Justin. Was that his sister?

Mortification swamped her. She shoved Justin's side. "Justin."

His eyes popped open. The alarm drained away and a lopsided smile graced his face. "Hey."

"I think Brigit's here."

He blinked and looked around. The mornings stayed dark longer this time of year, but the sun was up outside. "Did Isaiah sleep through the night?" His worry was back and he shot up. "Is he all right?"

They both peered into the baby monitor screen. Isaiah was wiggling around in his crib, letting out a small squawk every now and then.

The doctor in her had to reassure the frantic dad. "He's just fine." *What a night to pick to sleep through, kid.*

The creak of the front door resonated into the bedroom.

"Yo, Justin," Brigit called. "You home?"

A man's voice mumbled something. Caleb was here, too?

She wanted to dissolve into the bedding. Did everyone else get an audience when they finally decided to do something so out of character? And Justin's family, no less.

"No." Brigit sounded scandalized. Priya barely heard her whisper. "You think?"

Justin's chuckle was weak and his look apologetic. "Caleb must've spotted your car."

"Or my clothes all over the living room." The only time she didn't pick up after herself!

"Be right out," Justin called. He put a hand on her shoulder. She must look like she planned to dive out the window into refrigerator temps. "Do what you need to do in here. Help yourself to any of my clothes. I'll go talk to them and get Isaiah's bottle ready." He caught her eye. "We don't have to go into detail. They don't know it's your car and they won't tell anyone."

She inhaled a long breath. When she'd helped Justin with Isaiah's colic, she'd usually been gone before Brigit showed. She and Caleb shouldn't know whose car that was. But would it be so bad if people knew they were sleeping together?

Yes. She was sleeping with Maisy's ex, a *patient's* ex. Her clientele was 100 percent women. She'd lose their trust faster than it took to do a pelvic exam.

"They can't know I'm here." Her voice shook. "My job…"

Understanding dawned in his eyes. "I'll go out, grab your clothes and phone. Once they're out working sheep, I'll text you when it's all clear. Wait in here as long as you need."

She nodded, anxiety churning in her gut. He rolled out of

bed and grabbed a pair of pajama bottoms off the floor. Once he ducked out of the room, she collapsed back.

What a fine mess she'd gotten herself into. She almost —*almost*—regretted staying so long. But after all those orgasms, it was hard to. This benefits thing might have something to it. She'd never been so comfortable with a partner while at the same time being so exposed. Her legs had been twined around his head, his shoulders, his waist. She'd gone down on him with her ass in the air. And he'd insisted on having the light on. He liked to watch her.

Her belly flipped as she recalled the mix of intensity and wonder in his gaze. It made a girl feel powerful.

Had he been like that with all his exes? She'd always understood Maisy's infatuation, though she hadn't supported the obsession, but this uncovered another layer. And that other woman who'd used him? Perhaps Priya had her own obsession with him. After all, one night together and she was sitting in his bedroom naked, risking her job.

He popped back in with her clothes and phone. "Brigit's going to feed Isaiah while Caleb and I get stuff ready in the barn. When I see her outside and we're so far out into the pasture that they can't see you, I'll send you a message."

"Didn't they ask who was in here?"

He grinned. "Oh yeah. They're dying to know. But they're used to me not telling them a thing about my personal life."

He shucked his pants and started dressing in his work clothes. The faded jeans he pulled on only highlighted the muscles in his legs, and the long-sleeved Henley he pulled over his head draped over his chest more than she had last night. But the most devastatingly sweet thing he did was give her a quick kiss before darting back out the door.

She puffed her hair out of her face. Since she was trapped in here, she might as well shower. When she stood, she balled the sheets up and set them on his hamper. She found a fresh set at the top of his closet. She had to knock them down with a boot, but she succeeded and made his bed.

The shower was the quickest of her life. She wiped down the walls after and folded her towel over the hook when she was done. While she was killing time, she wiped down the counter and arranged his toiletries in the corner. As she dressed, she mused over the sharp turn her life had made in a day.

Had anything really changed? She was getting laid. She had to keep it secret. Beyond that, her parents and sister were traveling the world without her. Her grandparents in London still never came to see her, and her grandparents right here in Moore still worked all the time. At the clinic, she was still struggling to keep her patients.

So no. A few orgasms made her feel physically better, but she was still alone. At least she and Justin could stay friends. The only awkwardness this morning was thanks to his sister.

She sat on the bed and checked her phone. Nothing. Was Brigit outside yet? Perhaps Justin had forgotten.

Tiptoeing toward the closed bedroom door, she stayed quiet. Putting her ear close to the door, she listened. Her brain worked out a plan.

Brigit was either outside with Justin and had Isaiah with her. Or she'd put the baby in the crib and Justin had taken the monitor with him. The garage wasn't far away. But if Brigit was giving Isaiah his bottle, she was probably in the nursery. If she was in the rocking chair, she couldn't see where Priya parked. The window faced the wrong way.

She wasn't staying locked in this bedroom all morning while Justin went about his day. She had her weekly meals to prepare.

Cracking open the door, she slipped out and clicked it shut behind her. When she spun around, she yelped.

Brigit was tucked into the corner of the couch, facing the

nook that hid Justin's door. Her jaw dropped, but she didn't lower the bottle from Isaiah.

"Priya?" It came out as a near screech.

Priya flung her hand over her chest. "Don't give the doctor a heart attack."

"Sorry." Brigit blinked. The shadow her ball cap cast over her eyes did nothing to hide the woman's astonishment. She shook her head, her blond ponytail swinging from where it stuck out of the cap. "I was going to read Justin's fling the riot act. You know, be all overprotective sister, but I didn't expect you."

But I didn't expect you. Wasn't she Justin's type? "Who did you expect?"

The smirk on Brigit's face didn't feel personal, more like she knew what Priya was thinking. "Not someone who's emotionally stable, has a good job, is more educated than my brother, and didn't make insulting me her favorite sport growing up. No offense to Maisy, but her death doesn't change how she treated me."

Her irritation drained away. "No, I understand. Her behavior was escalating and we all denied it." She pushed a hand through her damp hair. "Listen, can you keep this to yourself? This thing is just casual, but if it gets out, it'll look bad."

"Because of Maisy?" Brigit shook her head. Isaiah turned his face from the bottle. She flipped a burp rag over her shoulder, set the bottle on the end table, and arranged Isaiah to pat his back.

"My work has been... It's been hard to..." Her throat tightened, and she couldn't finish. This was the second person she was talking to in as many days about her issue. She should be embarrassed by her failure as a doctor to gain her patients' trust, but she only wanted to talk about it. She wouldn't, though.

Brigit seemed to catch what she was alluding to. "This town can be brutal. Like a weird hive mind. Trying to change the impression that someone with boobs can't make ranching decisions hasn't been easy. I'm sure whenever anything bad happens to one of your patients, it's held against you much more than it would your dad."

Priya snorted. "Right? Though he's been practicing thirty years and I'm brand new, so I guess there's that." Though she also remembered Dad's hushed conversations with Mom about how he felt like an outsider and wasn't sure he could live in Moore. But he'd stuck it out. She couldn't go whining to him when he'd carved out a career long enough and successful enough that the clinic had hired his daughter.

"Whatever we can do to help, Priya. Say the word."

Priya gave her a wan smile. "Have you had a pap smear recently?"

Brigit's eyes widened, and she coughed out a laugh. "Well played, Dr. Patel. It's coming due. I'll keep you in mind."

No, she wouldn't, but Priya understood. It was hard to let a doctor you grew up with examine you and until recently, Brigit had thought Priya was a mean girl like Maisy. "I was just kidding."

Her gaze strayed to the door. She was a little too emotionally exposed to stay much longer.

"He's out in the barn with Caleb," Brigit said. She grinned when Isaiah let out a belch. "You might as well pop in before you go because I'm going to tell Caleb *everything*." Her smile turned reassuring. "But you can trust us. We know what it's like when the whole town gossips about your life."

Yeah, she'd pop in. Guess her awkward morning after was going to happen after all.

～

"Dude." Caleb snapped his fingers. His breath puffed out. The barn was protected from the wind but without the sun shining in and no sheep packed inside, it stayed chilly inside. "I lost you again. This mystery girl was that epic, huh?"

Justin glared at his friend, mostly to hide the fact that his night had in fact been that epic. Now he was fretting over the diminishing chances of it happening again, thanks to his sister and brother-in-law.

"So, about the sheep." They needed to be moved to new pastures before the snow got too deep for them to forage safely. The creatures might have a wool coat, but they were sensitive to the bitter wind chills Moore experienced in the winter. It was getting too close to Thanksgiving, but thanks to baby mania, they hadn't herded the sheep yet.

"Sure. The sheep." The corners of Caleb's eyes twinkled, but he hadn't pushed for the identity of the woman in Justin's bedroom. "Want me to distract Bridge so your girl can sneak out?"

"Could you?" Brigit would understand. Eventually. And while he didn't want to think about it as her brother, Caleb would know exactly what distracted Brigit.

The other man was about to answer when his gaze strayed to the door. A flurry of panting kicked up. The dogs were excited about someone's approach. The shock on his face told Justin exactly who it was.

He turned from where he was leaning against a metal stall rail. Priya picked her way through the dirt of the barn floor. Her pristine white winter coat was zipped to her chin and those fancy boots weren't her friend in this environment. The faint light streaming through the barn glistened off her recently washed hair.

She didn't look up as she spoke. "I should've listened to Brigit when she said suede wedge boots would die a slow death in the barn."

"There's no fresh manure," he replied. "As long as you stay out of the back. That's where we keep the injured sheep."

He wanted to go to her, give her a kiss and ask how she was doing. But friends didn't do that. They were casual. Looking at her didn't feel casual. His body heated enough to ward off all the cold. He could use a repeat of what they'd done as soon as Isaiah was down for the night.

So he played it cool and stayed standing by Caleb. Questions streamed through his mind. Had she grabbed breakfast? Was she dying inside? Had Brigit interrogated her? Had she been lured out of the room? He wouldn't have thought his twin would do that, but since she'd moved back to Moore, she'd been bolder in her words and actions. He liked it. Just not right now.

Priya stopped where she was. "I…don't want to ruin my boots." She stuffed her hands in her coat. "I, uh, just wanted to say bye."

He should walk her to her car. He wanted to. Dammit. This casual shit was messing with his mind. His flings when he was single had been just that. Temporary. With women who were looking for release as much as he was. He and Priya didn't quite fit into that category.

Besides, he didn't normally walk her out. And if he got too close to her, he might be the one ruining her boots. His own were filthy. He lifted his chin. "Call ya later?"

Her smile seemed forced. "Whenever."

As she tottered away, he wondered if their little show had been more for Caleb than for maintaining the limits of exclusive friends with benefits.

Caleb had the grace to wait until she was out of earshot before he spoke. "You and Priya, huh?"

"It's not like that."

"It's not like you were having a slumber party and her clothes were all over the living room?"

Justin rolled his eyes. "It's not serious. She knows I have a thing about getting into another relationship."

"But does she have a thing about it, too? Because if I recall correctly, the major issue between you and Maisy was that she wanted more than you. And then that lady in Denver wanted less than you."

"That's different." He stalked off to check his sick ewes. The ones he and Caleb had already looked at.

"How?" Caleb followed him. "Your bad experience on one end propelled you toward the other."

This was why he never talked about his personal life. "Friends with benefits. Ever hear of it?"

"Even the parts about how it turned out badly because one of the friends ends up wanting more."

Justin stopped and faced Caleb. The man wasn't laughing. He was genuinely concerned and not just for Justin. Priya had been on the periphery of their group of friends because he'd dated Maisy. Some of his ire drained away.

"Look, I'm not looking to debate. I slept with her. I want to do it again. But I don't want another woman pulling my strings to get me to do her bidding. She knows that, and all this"—he gestured between him and where Priya had walked out—"is between her and me. I'd appreciate it if you kept it all to yourself. She's having a hard time at work with what happened."

Caleb nodded. "I heard."

Justin cut him a sharp look.

His friend shrugged. "Firemen like to talk. One guy said his wife's friend convinced her to switch to a bigger clinic out of town. He says the drive is a pain in the ass and he's worried about the weather when the baby comes."

"That sucks."

"Yep. I tried sticking up for Priya, but he didn't need convincing. As firemen, we know freak shit happens. As ranchers, you and I know that animals get sick and die the second you turn your back. Humans aren't that much different." He shook his head, his dark eyes grim. "But not everyone is exposed to that."

They fell quiet for a moment, neither of them moving to do any work.

Then Caleb slapped him on the shoulder. "Maybe it's for the best. She didn't look cut out to be a rancher's wife." He swaggered toward the barn door.

Justin chuckled, but Caleb's words echoed in his head.

CHAPTER 10

The workday was almost done. Friday night was only a couple hours away. Despite that, Priya's optimism about the weekend was fading, along with her excitement over a new patient.

"I'm sorry, Anya, but I can't prescribe more hydrocodone." She faced the young woman that was as jittery as a…well, as an addict facing withdrawals. "Your prescription for that runs through your primary doctor."

Priya rattled off the options for endometriosis treatment, but her heart floated to the floor. The girl wasn't listening. Her case wasn't severe, but if she kept ignoring it and depending on pain meds, it would be.

Regardless, Priya went through her spiel. "Where would you like to start?"

"I'd like to start by dealing with the pain!" Anya jumped up. "I should've listened to what they said about you and gone to Dr. Bezos."

What had they said? And who was they?

Priya pursed her lips. Dr. Bezos. That part she understood. Also known as The Candy Man within the clinic. The conspiracy part of her wondered if he was spreading rumors about her and her abilities. When she'd first started, a quarter of his patients had switched to her, but she'd quickly learned that many were looking for a young, inexperienced doctor to give them another pain med prescription.

It hadn't taken long for them to realize that Priya monitored their current prescriptions and was more interested in treating the reason for the pain than doling out more pills and calling it a day. The medications were a tool, not a cure.

She'd talked to her superior about The Candy Man already. Then the tragedy with Maisy had happened and she hadn't had enough patients to fight over.

Anya paced the tiny room. She hadn't stalked out. Priya took it as a good sign.

"Anya. The pain is going to get so bad that your current prescription won't be effective. It'll get so bad that no amount of pain killer will dent it."

The girl paused, chewing the index fingernail of one hand, her other arm curved around her abdomen.

Priya again suggested a treatment plan. Anya listened. She probably still planned to get more pills out of another doctor, but she also wanted her condition treated. Priya could work with that.

The appointment wrapped up and Priya walked the woman out. Back at the nurse's station, only Krista remained.

"That went better than I thought." She squeezed the hand sanitizer nozzle to fill her palm with foam.

"There'll be more next week."

Priya groaned. Thanksgiving was next week. Dr. Bezos was out of the office until the Monday after. She grabbed a sanitizing wipe and started wiping counters. It was standard for end of shift, but she needed soothing. "At least my schedule will be sort of full." She raised a questioning brow. She'd been too afraid to look.

"It's better than it's been. Not many openings left for each day. We'll have to live it up."

Oh, she would. An entire week of not worrying about the clinic administrator calling her into her office.

Priya glanced at Krista. Would she know what Anya was talking about? "Hey, have you heard anyone saying things about me? Warning patients to stay away?"

Krista frowned. "No. But most people know I'm your nurse. In my baby-wearing classes, they've already had their babies. Why?"

"Just something Anya said. It was kind of weird."

Krista lifted a brow. "Was she high?"

"No, and that was part of her problem with me."

"Maybe that's what she meant. Someone told her you wouldn't hook her up. They can't put a quarter in you and turn the knob like they can with him. What can you do?"

Exactly. The guy had been working here longer than her dad. He had power and connections and the rest of the staff knew it. So why couldn't she escape the feeling that wasn't what Anya had meant?

"Whatcha got plans for tonight?" Krista asked.

"Not much." So much. Her parents were coming home tomorrow, so she was sleeping over at Justin's tonight. She'd have the rest of the weekend to reconnect with Mom and Dad and hear about their trip.

She hadn't seen Justin all week, and each night was more restless than the last. Her body wanted more of what he gave.

"I bet it'll be quiet with your parents gone for another week," Krista said as she organized her desk for the night. "What are you doing for Thanksgiving with them out of town?"

She frowned, the wet wipe hanging in her hand. "What do

you mean?" Mom had told her not to worry about the airport pickup. Priya assumed that meant she'd call a cab.

"The surprise trip? The one I heard your mom's been planning for months?"

Priya couldn't bring herself to shake her head. How did Krista know more than she did?

Her humiliation was averted when Krista explained. "I guess she arranged for his schedule to be kept clear this week so she could surprise him with an extra week in Mexico, complete with deep-sea fishing."

Right. Because her vegetarian father made an exception for fish he caught.

Krista sighed wistfully. "Those are the perks of being here for thirty years. They have a little pull. You didn't know?"

She forced a smile. "I guess Mom thought I was five again and couldn't keep a secret."

"Isn't that like parents? You have a med school degree and they still act like you don't know how to tie your shoes."

Priya somehow managed to laugh, but she was hurting inside. With the flurry before the trip, Mom had probably forgotten to mention the surprise.

She pulled out her phone and sent a message to Devya. *Did you know that Mom is surprising Dad with an extra week in Mexico?*

Who knew what time it was in Paris? Priya didn't bother to check. Ordinarily she would've been considerate, but her blood pressure thrummed between her ears. If Devya knew, then… Well, that'd really suck.

She walked out with Krista and did all the perfunctory actions expected of her. The "have a good weekend" routine, complete with a smile and a wave. But when she got into her car, she slumped in her seat.

Her phone buzzed. It was Devya. *Soooo exciting!*

That wasn't a clear answer, but it was clear enough.

Devya called Mom all the time. She was the little princess. The one they worried about.

No, it was okay. It was fine to be the responsible kid. She hadn't run to them crying on their shoulders when Emmett had dumped her. Her plans had been set and she'd followed through even though her heart had been breaking.

Being a free-spirited artist meant Devya was treated differently, and Priya accepted that. Was still trying to accept that.

Her phone rang. She fumbled with it but answered. "Dev? Is everything okay?"

Loud music almost drowned out her sister's voice. "Of course, why wouldn't it be?"

"Isn't it the middle of the night there?" She winced as she said it. That was a ripe opening for her sister's teasing.

Devya's throaty laugh was so like her. "The night is just starting, Pri-Pri. I miss your face and thought I'd call before" —a knowing giggle—"the night gets away from me."

Priya did a quick calculation. It was almost midnight in Paris. Oh, to be young and funded by doting parents and grandparents. "I didn't know about Mom and Dad. I thought they were coming home tomorrow."

"Old people can be spontaneous. In fact, you should try it sometime."

Devya's teasing got old. Priya could afford to party all night, too, if she hadn't directed all her financial help into paying for school.

"Guess what? I'm flying to London next week. Papa Patel didn't want me to get homesick over Thanksgiving."

Tears pricked the backs of Priya's eyes. Her grandfather who didn't celebrate Thanksgiving and never visited for the holiday when he'd lived in America was going to recognize the day for Devya. Why had she answered the phone? "Tell them—" She had to clear her throat. "Tell them hi for me."

"I will. I should let you go. I'm probably keeping you from exciting weekend plans."

Her weekend was wide-open now. "No. I'll probably help Justin Walker with his new baby." She squeezed her eyes. Why had she said that? It would inspire questions.

"Oooh, Justin." Another laugh that proved Devya lived life at full speed. "I would ask if he was anyone a sister should have to worry about, but *come on.*"

Priya glared out the window. "What do you mean?"

"You? Like, a rancher's wife? Living out in the country? With animals that walk in their own poo? Pri-Pri. You'd go crazy." There was that laugh again, only it was at Priya's expense. "You wear leather, you don't grow it."

"He raises sheep."

"And you prefer cashmere. That's goat wool, FYI."

Enough of this. "We're just friends, and he needs a hand."

"As long as he's not using you." Her spontaneous sister was suddenly serious. "Promise me you're going to do something this weekend that *you* need. Take care of yourself for once."

She flashed back to the moment she'd told Devya that Emmett had broken up with her. *Good. Now you can do something for yourself instead of what Emmett always needs.*

Her baby sister surprised her sometimes. "I promise."

"I miss you." Devya sighed wistfully as a new round of music started. "I don't miss Moore, but I miss you. And Mom and Dad. Grandma and Grandpa."

Priya frowned at the longing in those words. Suddenly, she was grateful Papa Patel was looking out for Devya. But that was how it worked. They all worried about Dev. "Give Papa and Nana a big hug—for me and for yourself."

"Yes— Oh, my friends are here. Bye!"

The line went dead. Priya stared at the phone. *You? Like, a rancher's wife?* She'd ignore Devya's comment but not the rest of her advice. Do something for herself.

That would be spending the night with Justin. That should qualify because of their deal. He wasn't using her. They were using each other.

~

HE SHOULD BE IRRITATED.

Priya was on her knees, that beautiful hair spilling out of a messy bun and caressing her neck, her pert ass in the air, giving him a look as wicked as the one he'd been graced with the night before.

He made sure his expression told her exactly what he thought of her position. "Rub it hard, baby."

She laughed but didn't miss a beat as she scoured the bathtub. He gave it a good wipe every… Well, he didn't have a schedule, but he didn't live in filth.

He'd just come back inside from fixing a busted corral in the barn. Isaiah was cooing in his bouncy chair outside the bathroom and Priya was cleaning.

"Is everything all right?" He thought she would go home on Saturday, but she'd mentioned plans with her parents falling through. Some surprise trip.

Last weekend, he'd only had one short night with her. It was Sunday, and he enjoyed having her around way too much. But when she got up in her head, the cleaning supplies came out.

"Fine."

"Uh-huh. That's why you wiped down the entire kitchen yesterday and dusted both floors of the house." A cute little furrow developed between her brows and he kept going. "You should talk, or next week I might unleash you on the basement."

Her scowl turned to a playful glare. "I like cleaning."

He should walk away. She didn't want to talk to him. Fine. But her evasiveness curdled in his gut. "Do you like it, or does it become an itch you have to scratch?"

She sat back on her heels, her blue-rubber-gloved hands hanging over the edge of the tub. Whatever she was using didn't fume up the place. He'd have to get pointers from her. "It's an itch. You got me."

He folded his arms and leaned against the doorframe. "What I don't get is why you're like the CIA about it. We're friends."

She lifted a shapely brow. "Want to talk about what happened in Denver?"

Touché. Her challenge was too hard to pass up. He should just bypass the subject, but...he couldn't. His curiosity about his friends wasn't usually so strong. "Denver. Okay. It started in college. Still in Denver. I met Gabrielle. She had an entrepreneurial spirit, and my weaknesses in business were her strengths. We created a little marketing startup."

Priya peeled off her gloves and dropped them in the tub before folding herself on the floor. Isaiah was content. Justin didn't plan to go to into too much detail. That'd be humiliating. But the twist of the knife was all he needed to recollect. Not the hints that his country-boy persona was a hindrance and Gabrielle's offer to shop with him. Her encouragement no matter how high the price tag. Or the way she chided him about how he said "ain't" occasionally.

"Our first accounts were campus clubs, done for nearly free. But we used them to promote ourselves, and people bought into the millennial new grads who could do the same work for better, faster, and cheaper than the others." Gabrielle's networking had been first-rate. Probably still was. With her new fiancé and business partner. "We were skyrocketing to the top of our field. We hired assistants, paid benefits. And we were even older than our employees."

Interest came off Priya in waves. He didn't want to keep talking. To see that pride she harbored for him fade.

"We broke up. 'Better business partners than bed partners,' she said. Then when a headhunter from a firm in Texas contacted me, we got back together." Only at the time, he'd been too naïve to connect the dots. Gabrielle hadn't completely changed the country boy in him. "Sound familiar?"

"It's okay not to give up on someone, Justin."

She would say that. His passionate, considerate woman. Friend. "But we kept the company strong through another breakup. Every time I thought about the future and it wasn't in Denver doing her bidding, she lured me back in."

The travel. The parties. The isolation. He hadn't known the people he signed paychecks for. As Gabrielle's fetch dog, he'd been on the go constantly. He'd missed his family and he'd missed farming and ranching.

Priya cocked her head, the hair from her messy topknot spilling to the side of her face. "How did you break free?"

He didn't offer up a clarification for her. Break free? No. He'd been replaced. "She found someone else who was already at the top, not clawing his way there. Divorced. Grown kids. CEO. We sold the company and…" He lifted his shoulders. "Here I am."

"So when you called Maisy up, that was when you found out this Gabrielle was engaged, or when the company papers were final?"

Shame slicked a sour patch down his throat. He swallowed, but it didn't help. "The sale was final. I had to keep traveling back until it was over. That was when she wore the ring." And Gabrielle had driven away in her new Lexus. The company that had bought out his? Her new fiancé owned it.

He'd been thoroughly duped.

"What was your company called?"

"Loud Paint." At her incredulous expression, he explained, "Her idea." He'd had no say. "Trendy, I guess." Now that she was mollified, he pushed. "Your turn."

She huffed a hunk of hair out of her eyes. The look on her face was exactly how he'd felt when he told his story. Just when he thought she wouldn't live up to her end of the deal, she spoke. "It sounds so insignificant compared to what you went through. My parents didn't tell me they were going to be gone an extra week."

He bobbed his head. Annoying. But enough to rage clean his house?

"The whole clinic knew, though. And Devya."

"Isn't she in France?"

She nodded once. "Paris."

"Ah." That explained more of it. Ouch.

"And Devya." She waved her hand like she could conjure a word out of thin air. "They all coddle her. All of them. But still, my problems don't compare to yours."

He mulled over what she'd said. She was downplaying how much it hurt her. She'd probably cooked and cleaned for her family, and they'd jetted off to the tropics. The slight seemed minimal until she looked around and had no one to talk to. "You've made it your career to heal people. Who do you go to when you need to talk?"

The flash of stark vulnerability in her eyes floored him. He'd hit the bull's-eye and she hadn't been ready. Her eyes glistened. "There was a group in college. I keep in touch, through social media and stuff, but we're all over the country." Her expression darkened, and he sensed another story there. Had she told anyone that one? "Maisy…had her issues. But I could talk to her. Kind of."

"And she'd just say fuck them and talk about herself?"

A laugh sputtered out of her. "Right. But oddly enough, it made me feel better."

He wasn't prepared for his next question, but it left his lips before he'd thought about it. "Did she tamper with the condom?"

~

JUSTIN'S DEMEANOR changed with his question. Anxiety churned in her belly. How did she answer? They were opening up to each other, like real friends. Forget the sex. She wanted someone to talk to. The way Justin glossed over what Gabrielle had done to him—and he was lying to himself if he thought for one minute that he'd done anything more than skim the surface—it was probably still more than he'd told anyone else. She didn't miss the shame in his eyes. He hated how he'd succumbed to this Gabrielle.

And Priya had never told anyone about how insignificant she felt in her own family. Not even Maisy. Justin was right. Whenever she'd broached a personal issue, Maisy had rolled her eyes and said, "Fuck them." The cavalier response had validated her feelings, regardless.

What did she owe Maisy? Would the truth hurt or help?

If she lied, she might lose his trust, but what Maisy had told her had been in the confidence of her office. Yet, Maisy was gone, and he should know the truth.

But as she met Justin's gaze, the truth retreated from her lips. His stony blue gaze sent her pulse rate higher. He'd gone from betrayed heartbreak to cold as ice.

"I...don't think so." She pushed the stray locks of her hair out of her eyes with the back of her hand. Maisy had tampered with the truth of the situation, so not technically a lie. No. It was a lie. "Do you have reason to suspect she did?"

"Yeah. Just because that's the way she was." He shifted his

gaze out the door to where Isaiah had gone quiet in his bouncy chair. "I love my son. I don't wish for him not to have happened, but it would suck if the decision had been taken from me."

She used the side of the tub to stand up, wanting to fold herself into him. To chase away the trouble in his gaze. His body was stiff and his expression distant. Did he know she was lying? "I keep telling myself she would've gotten help after he was born."

Justin's dubious gaze returned to her. "She was stubborn. Her ear had to be killing her." She winced at his choice of words. Her infection *had* killed her. "I can't believe she didn't go in. Simple antibiotics."

Priya nodded. He needed to talk about Maisy and what had happened, but at the same time, there wasn't much to say.

"You know, in high school, she came on to me. I think that's why I stayed with her. She made it easy."

He laughed at her expression. The tense air between them evaporated. "Sorry. That was the last thing I expected you to say."

"Nah." His humor faded. "She made life a lot harder as an adult. But as a teenager, she set the pace and I was along for the ride. If she got mad and broke up with me, then I hung out with Caleb more. Dated other girls, which never failed to bring her back."

"Like clockwork." They'd go to a football game or pasture party, see another girl clinging to his side, and Maisy would lose her shit. "I think that's why her tactics changed so dramatically when you moved back. Once you showed interest again, she thought it was finally time for you two to be together forever."

He closed his eyes, leaning back on his hands against the counter. "I sometimes wonder… Was she panicking because I wouldn't commit and she was having a baby and— Well, if she was super sick, I'd have to stick around to take care of her, right?" The muscles of his neck strained like he was trying not to say his next words. "Did she die because of me?"

"Justin, no." She crossed to him, not caring if she smelled like citrus cleaner and rubber gloves. Wrapping her arms around his shoulders, she laid her head on his broad chest. He released his grip on the edge of the counter and wrapped his arms around her. "I know it'll be hard, but you can't blame yourself."

Blame me. I failed Maisy.

The rumble of his voice vibrated against her cheek. "I'm so damn glad I get to raise Isaiah and not have to fight anyone to see him or worry about his safety. But I'm not glad she's gone. Not like that, not at all. It's… It's a fucked-up place to be. How the hell do I explain that to Isaiah when he's older?"

For the first and maybe only time, she was glad she'd lied. It'd be easier for Justin to heal. She leaned her head back to look at him. "By saying what feels right. Your family and Maisy's family only want what's best for him. We'll follow your lead." Her breath froze in her lungs. She'd naturally included herself in his group, and in Isaiah's future.

He stared at her for a few moments. Her throat burned. She was holding her breath. Slowly, she sucked in new air.

"You're right," he finally said. A glow sparked to life inside of her. He hadn't denied her role in his life, and for once she dared hope there could be more for them in the future. Until what he said next dumped a bucket of ice on that feeling. "But it's the reason why I'm done with relationships. I gotta concentrate on what's best for me and my son."

CHAPTER 11

*J*ustin bit back his curse when his passenger reached for the door handle without waiting for him. He threw the vehicle in park and killed the engine. "Gram. I'll be right around."

She was a wily one. With her walker, she could outpace any of her grandkids, all who towered over her. He got out and rushed over to her side. Gram clung to the door while he unfolded her walker.

Thanksgiving dinner was over, visiting was done, and evening approached. He'd gone to Travis's house. Brigit and Caleb had picked up Grandma Agnes and he'd offered to bring her back to the nursing home.

"You're such a dear, but it's getting late." She was already wheeling off before he'd unhooked the baby carrier from the base in the backseat. "But I sure do appreciate the ride. And the invite. This old lady doesn't get out much."

He grinned, walking behind her with the carrier hanging in one hand. Between him, his cousins, and his aunts and uncles, Gram probably had a more active social life than he did. "Anytime."

He held the door open for her, planning to visit for a few minutes until she was settled. The nursing home was at least ten degrees warmer than he kept his house. In her room, Gram removed her thin jacket and hung it up in her closet. Her moves were precise, the slight shake in her hands not slowing her down.

"I sure enjoy being surrounded by kids again. Your little guy and Travis's little boy are going to be thick as thieves. Just you wait."

"I've got it coming, according to Mom and Dad."

Gram pushed her walker into a corner and eased herself into her favorite chair. It was the same one he remembered her having as a kid. "Oh, what's this?"

A cupcake rested on her end table. Justin's interest was riveted to the pink and green frosting.

"Vanilla bean," a woman said from the doorway. One of the nurses. Gram smiled and waved her in, but she shook her head and smiled. "I'll come back when your company's gone. I just wanted to tell you that if you don't want it, I'll have it."

Gram chuckled. "That good, huh? Who's spoiling us?"

"So yummy. I guess the cupcake fairy swung by this afternoon and passed them out." The nurse's face sobered. "It was a real pick-me-up for the residents who didn't have anywhere to go. The cafeteria's pumpkin pie only goes so far."

Justin hung on every word. Vanilla bean cupcakes with pink and green frosting. What were the odds? When had Priya made the time to do this on Thanksgiving?

His stomach hit bottom like it was full of horseshoes. Her parents and sister were out of the country. The Saunders lived in town, but what if they hadn't invited her over? No, he couldn't see that happening. But Priya's mom wasn't an only child. What if the Saunders had gone out of town? Priya wasn't the type to latch on to anyone, to tell them she had no one to spend the holiday with.

And any family that lived close was probably like him and had assumed she had plans.

"That was so sweet of our mystery guest." Gram rocked in her chair.

"Very," said the nurse. "Lucille next door is a patient of hers and told us who our cupcake fairy was. Dr. Patel hung around and visited with a few people."

"Oh yes." Gram pegged him with her sharp gaze, like her grandma radar was going off and she knew he was way too interested in this conversation for it to be about cupcakes or someone's goodwill. "Do you know her?"

"She's a friend of mine." The extremely inappropriate and ill-timed image of her hair hanging over her bare shoulders and tickling her breasts flashed through his head. The temperature of the place rose another ten degrees. "Priya. Yeah, a friend."

"Mm-hmm." Gram might as well have said bullshit. "I thought one of the Patel girls was your age."

The nurse's gusty sigh broke in. "I'll give up my not-so-subtle begging for the cupcake." She looked at Justin. "But seriously, if you see her, tell her thank you and anytime. Literally. Anytime. We don't turn sweets away."

"Do you?" Gram asked when the other woman left. "See her at all?"

"She, uh, helped me a lot when Isaiah had colic." He was reverting to the kid who couldn't bluff Gram about how the shop window got busted.

"That's what I thought your dad said. She's a doctor?"

He had to put a stop to Gram's inquiries. The nursing home grapevine burned hot. "She is. But I'm not looking for a relationship." He hefted the baby carrier to prove his point.

"You don't have to be looking for a relationship if it finds you first."

"Thanks, Gram." Isaiah squawked. It was getting close to bottle time and Justin was living on the edge as it was by leaving the diaper bag in the pickup.

"You need to get him home. Thanks again, Justin."

He leaned over to kiss her, then lifted the carrier so she could say goodbye to Isaiah. "I'll try to stop by again this weekend. The boy and I are getting out of the house more."

As he walked outside, he couldn't help but look for signs that Priya had been there, or maybe was still around. But she wasn't. It was almost seven. Isaiah's bedtime was soon.

Soon, but not yet.

Was she home?

Last Thanksgiving, Brigit had stormed out of the house when she'd realized Caleb was spending the holiday alone. Their relationship had turned a corner that weekend. But Justin wasn't looking for one. And he didn't want one to find him.

Still, he'd be a shitty friend if he drove home knowing she was by herself, after he'd spent the day with his siblings and their spouses and his niece and nephew. Last year, his twin had refused to let someone close to her be alone for a family holiday, while Justin had relaxed and watched football with Dad. He couldn't do that to Priya.

Isaiah let out another half cry. His early warning wail that he'd better get a bottle or he was getting loud.

"Don't worry, kiddo. We'll get you your bottle a little sooner than expected."

HEADLIGHTS FLASHED through the sitting room. Priya frowned and unfolded herself from the couch. She'd been doing nothing but staring at the article about a doula's place in the C-section surgery. Baking had gotten her through today. Now she needed to work on finding light reading material.

The adjustment from full-time student to full-time doctor was hard to move beyond, not to mention the drive to be the best doctor possible. Dad's words of wisdom were suddenly…wise. *Your entire life can't be about being a doctor. It's only part of what you are. Remember to keep the Fs in your life. Family. Friends. Fun.*

Her family was all out of town. Her friends were minimal. The fun part was easier to work on but still so difficult.

Wandering to the front door, she jumped as the doorbell rang through the place.

Who could be here?

She didn't have to wonder long. The tall man with a baby carrier standing outside the door was more than familiar. Tingles traveled down her spine.

Justin was here. She opened the door. "Is everything all—"

"Gram wanted to thank you for the cupcakes." He stood on the welcome mat. His black parka was one she didn't see him wear often. It definitely wasn't the brownish work coat he usually wore. A blue fleece with green tractors on it covered the baby carrier.

"Oh. It was no problem." She stepped back to let him in. He knew she'd been to the home to deliver treats. Did he know why? "I thought A. Walker might be your grandma." The full names weren't on the placards outside the door.

"She is. Hey, Isaiah needs a bottle. Mind if I feed him?"

"Not at all." She brushed away the tendril of disappointment. He'd come here to feed Isaiah, not see her, but she was happy to see them both. It'd been a long, lonely day.

She took his coat while he stepped out of his boots.

"Help yourself in the kitchen," she said. Pointing to the

sitting room where she'd left the light on, she picked up the carrier. "I'll be in there after I get Isaiah out."

Noting how nice it felt to have these two guys in her quiet house, she firmly reminded herself not to get used to it. *I'm done with relationships* still rang in her ears. She distracted herself by unbuckling the wiggling baby and cooing at him.

When Justin entered the sitting room, he eyed the medical journal on the coffee table. "Exciting reading material?"

"Actually, right before you arrived, I'd come to the conclusion that I needed to find a lighter read." She held her hand out for the bottle.

"You sure? I don't think I've fed him one bottle today. Not after the morning one anyway."

She wasn't only doing it to help him. It wasn't like she could cuddle, rock, feed, and bathe Isaiah all these weeks without growing attached. She didn't miss just Justin all week, but she couldn't admit that. He might think she was trying to manipulate him.

"Have a seat." She relaxed as Isaiah drank. Justin dropped into the padded wicker chair across from her. As the seat creaked he lifted his hands and looked down like he was afraid he'd wrecked it. "You didn't hurt anything. Mom likes her wicker. You should see our porch set."

He shot her a quick grin and looked around, spending extra time on the photos from her childhood trips to India to visit relatives. Then he moved on to Dad's plaques hanging on one wall. Her mother's were on another. Priya and Devya shared an "I love me" wall, but there was nothing current on it. All of Priya's stuff hung in her office and on her clinic walls. For how much longer, she didn't know.

The week had been brutal. What should've revived her had drained her in a depressing way. More cancellations. The ones who'd followed through, Dr. Bezos's patients, were not kind, and with each one, she'd felt like she was undergoing some test she didn't know the rules for.

"Was that your Thanksgiving?" Justin's gaze was on her. She had to look away.

"Grandma and Grandpa Saunders are in Fergus Falls with my aunt." She had called her grandparents and asked what they had planned for today, but she hadn't mentioned that she had no invites. Aunt Dana probably would've invited her, but a girl had her pride. Begging an invitation to a family gathering sucked.

"So you baked cupcakes and made Lucille's day by hanging out with her."

"Her family's in Florida." At her appointment last week, Lucille had mentioned that she'd be spending her Thanksgiving working. There'd been nothing to clean this morning, so Priya had baked three batches of cupcakes and driven to the nursing home. "It's funny, though. I wouldn't have thought twice about others who were alone for the holiday if I weren't in the same boat."

"How come you didn't say anything last weekend?"

"Didn't seem like a big deal." Said the girl who'd had a good sob after she'd put the first batch of cupcakes in the oven. Besides, what did he think he could've done about it? Brought her along to his brother's? What would people think?

Her thought was a bit too sarcastic. She had to stop the budding bitterness. She had entered this arrangement with eyes wide-open. He had a reason for his mistrust and she had a reason to hide their connection.

His gaze stayed on her, like he was waiting for more.

"How was your Thanksgiving?" she asked.

His scrutiny dissolved in a grin. "Good. We brought Gram over. It was fun. I felt like my old self again. But with a baby."

"I hear the same things from moms. Those first few months, they're in a baby fog, but then they get a moment of feeling like their old selves and it's like they move into a new phase of life." Was he moving into a new phase? "How's your family?"

While she finished feeding and burping Isaiah, he rambled on about how well his family was doing. The baby fell asleep. She glanced at the mariner clock on the wall. It was his normal bedtime.

"I think you're in trouble," she murmured. "He's asleep."

"I had planned it so I could drop Gram off and get home in time to give him a bottle before bed. But you were the talk of the nursing home."

She filled in what he didn't say. He'd realized she was alone today and had come by. Her day had turned out well. The morning had been rough while she whiled away her time in self-pity, but once the talk with Lucille had inspired her, she'd rallied. The nursing home trip had been fun, even if she'd had to give herself a pep talk to actually walk into the home. Would they want anything she baked? Had her reputation spread that far? But the older population comprised only a small percentage of her patient base—and hadn't shrunk over the last year.

"I think I need to make it a tradition," she said. "Lots of Dad's patients asked about him and remembered stories he'd told of me."

More importantly, she'd learned that she'd been too dependent on her family to pave the way for her. She needed to unbutton her lab coat herself and find her own people to hang out with, and if they were eighty, who cared? Her coworkers had tentatively extended invitations to her.

Why had she never accepted?

Because Maisy had been in the later stages of pregnancy

and freaking out about not being able to pin Justin down. Then there'd been Justin.

And there was still Justin. If she made more friends, real friends she didn't sleep with, would this thing between them satisfy her? Would he leave once she said she wanted more?

"I should get him home." Justin paused, as if it were a question.

It was on the tip of her tongue to tell him to stay. To find a way to make a safe place for Isaiah to sleep, or heck, to offer to go home with him.

But it felt like a cop-out. No matter how good he looked sitting across from her, or how many times he could make her orgasm, she needed to round out this day. She'd woken up alone and she was going to bed alone.

As he packed up the bottle and loaded Isaiah into his seat, a sense of pride descended over her like a cozy blanket. If she could find her own way in her personal life, she'd find her own professionally—and get to the bottom of why she was losing patients.

And when she'd managed that, then...she'd face this friends-with-benefits thing, and whether they wanted to keep going as they were or go on a real date. Or break it off entirely.

ustin rolled over and kissed the bare shoulder peeking out from under the blankets. He grinned when Priya groaned and burrowed closer.

He propped his head on his hand. They'd made it through Christmas without seeing each other much, but neither of them had gotten the other a gift. She'd tentatively double-checked that gift giving wasn't expected between them. He'd reassured her that he didn't have a present. Never once had he and Caleb exchanged gifts, and Caleb was his best friend.

For this holiday, he'd made sure she had family to be with. She'd spent it at her grandparents' place in town with her mom and dad. Justin's parents had flown in, and his entire family had gotten together at Travis's. As soon as their routine had resumed, she'd been back in his bed. They were both still on the same page. Just friends who had amazing sex together.

He rubbed her shoulder. "You mind if I go out and do chores?"

"You mean do I mind if you go out and beat Brigit to it?"

He grinned at the lump she made under the covers, only her pile of black hair blooming out like a midnight-colored rose. Yanking the blankets off sounded like a good idea, but she was naked under there. When they had sex it was the only time she slept without clothes on and that was only if it was a vigorous night.

Last night had been especially vigorous. Something about work was bothering her, but she hadn't said much beyond "I wish some coworkers were still on vacation."

But he'd reaped the benefits. He couldn't complain. He *shouldn't* complain. It was just… They'd been doing this for weeks, and had been leaning on each other for longer, but she still didn't confide in him. Since Thanksgiving, they were back to superficial discussions while they drank wine. About Isaiah. And oddball cases that strolled into her office. His siblings and their families. Then they had sex. Deep and meaningful had been taken off the table.

As long as she talked to someone, that was what mattered. Last weekend, she'd gone out with work buddies, and while he'd missed his time with her, he'd been happy. The next night, she'd come over. Back to their arrangement.

He rolled out of bed. The Priya bump under the covers didn't twitch. She was asleep again.

He glanced at the baby monitor. It was early yet. Isaiah had had a bottle four hours ago and would probably be waking up soon.

Dressing as quietly as possible, he tiptoed out to the kitchen. The batch of muffins Priya had baked last night rested on the counter. He wolfed down four and just as stealthily made his way outside.

He was in the barn, shoveling feed into the trough for the sick ewes and weak young lambs he had sequestered, when the familiar rumble of Caleb's pickup cut through the air. A few minutes later, the crunch of Caleb's footsteps announced his approach.

He lifted his chin. "Morning."

"I should learn to turn right around when I see Pri's car in the drive. You're always out here by the time I park." Caleb grinned. A black stocking hat was pulled down to his eyebrows, but the white crescent-shaped Cruise ranch logo Brigit had designed stuck out loud and proud. His hands were shoved in his jacket, probably with the gloves he wasn't wearing. "Brigit's here, too, but she went into the house."

Priya was probably awake by now, used to Caleb and Brigit's intrusion into their morning. She now made sure all traces of their clothing and any blankets they used under them were gone.

Each time, she was content to stay inside where it was warm. He came out here and did his thing, and she wrinkled her nose at his dirty clothes when he went back inside. He'd probably do the same thing if he went to the hospital and saw her immediately after aiding in a birth. Their worlds were different, but out in the middle of nowhere, they collided nicely.

To give him something else to mull over besides how comfortable this routine had gotten, he gestured to the freeze-proof water tank in front of him. "This is the best investment I've ever made."

"This winter is going to tax how well it can keep water from freezing." Caleb came to a stop next to him. "Brigit said your mom asked about Priya. That you mentioned her a few times."

"I did?" He tried to recall his recent conversations with Mom.

"With you, it only takes mentioning a woman's name once for Joan to think there's something more there."

Justin scowled at the round tank in front of him. Two

ewes munched at the trough and a six-month-old lamb limped around his boots and nudged his leg. "What'd Brigit say?"

"That you were just friends and you needed a little help with Isaiah once in a while." Caleb chuckled and shoved his hands in his coat pockets. "I'm sure she was disappointed. Someone like Priya would make her a happy mother-in-law, definitely more than me or Kami did at first."

"She adores Kami, and I think sometimes you're her favorite son."

Caleb's grin was full of mischief. He reveled in how "Mama Walker" doted on him. "I'll never compare to her little boys, but it doesn't mean I don't like how she brags about me to everyone—after she's covered the successes of her own kids, of course."

Justin had never given his mother much fodder to talk about. He'd intended to, of course, when he'd charged out into the world to prove himself. The few times he called home though, he would mention where he was traveling and only that he was working on a big account. Not that it was a million-dollar merger between two marketing companies and his company would only come out on top if he did his job correctly. He would never mention that the company he worked for was half his. He had never felt like it.

The pressure. The gnawing stress. The headaches and heartburn he formed at only twenty-five years old. All so he could fill someone else's bank account and have his contribution to the effort lost in the small print. He hadn't been in it for the prestige, but he'd expected more. More fulfillment. More pride in what he did. More rewards that weren't really more work in disguise, like the meet and greets in Aspen. Not a real vacation.

Guys ten years older than him were taking blood pressure medication and going through divorces. He'd thought he could escape that future.

Until Gabrielle had strung him along and his nights of sleep had been cut in half as he ran numbers and created proposals. He'd thought then that they were blistering hot between the sheets, but only because of the lies she'd fed him. Like that he was the only one. She'd confide in him about personal problems with her family, whom he'd never met, so he would double down and work harder to compensate. She'd played on his emotions when he'd been replaceable in so many ways.

"So is there?" Caleb's questions hauled him out of his dark memories.

"Is there what?"

"More."

Justin laughed. "No. I told you how it is. We're both adults."

"Uh-huh."

Justin crossed his arms. He was not having this conversation. "I'm standing in sheep shit, covered in muck. Have you ever seen Priya's house?"

Caleb's wry smile answered his question. "I'm only in Lakewood for emergencies. There's literally no other reason for me to be in that neighborhood."

"Then you can see why we're not in a relationship. It'd be like trying to build a castle in the swamp." And he wasn't trading his swamp for marble columns. He turned around. Caleb would get the signal that this conversation was done.

So maybe Priya keeping to herself was a good thing. She didn't make promises that she had no plans to keep and she wasn't trying to change him. He had no interest in climbing any corporate ladders, just a regular one to repair a leaky barn roof. Working for his family, being accepted for himself instead of what he could be changed into, was all he wanted. Any woman who tried to alter his little patch of paradise would have to leave.

~

IF ANYONE HAD TOLD her that she'd be lounging in Justin Walker's living room, chatting with his twin sister like they'd been besties since they were toddlers, Priya might have never left Moore.

Which wouldn't have been a good thing. Neither was her crush on Justin when her best friend had been hot and heavy with him. She'd gone off, gotten her education, and always planned to settle back down in Moore and do the whole family thing. She'd done all that without being guaranteed a shot with Justin.

Her life hadn't revolved around a man then and it didn't now.

But maybe she wanted it to. A tiny bit. Her world didn't have to revolve around a guy, just travel next to it.

Which was kind of what it was doing. But for how much longer? Was there a length of time past which it wouldn't look bad to announce she had feelings for him?

"I heard something the other day." Brigit stopped cooing at Isaiah and directed her bright gaze at her. Isaiah cart-wheeled his legs and looked around.

"Oh?" Priya curled her legs under herself. A pit cracked open in her stomach. Brigit wasn't one to gossip and this sounded serious.

Brigit opened her mouth, then closed it again and gave Priya a hard look. "I know you can keep stuff quiet. Patient-doctor confidentiality. Can you do that with what I'm about to tell you?"

"Of course."

"Caleb and I want to start a family soon."

Priya grinned. She'd heard this phrase so often, but the excitement for the couple never faded. Not in this stage. There were plenty of bumps in the road and potential heartache later. But she'd learned early to celebrate this moment of unadulterated optimism. "Congratulations."

Brigit's smile was almost shy. "Thanks. I don't want word to get out and then have family and friends constantly watching and waiting for an announcement. I'd rather wait until we're a few months into baking the bun in the oven."

"Understandable." The crack yawned open further. This was getting into Priya's territory and Brigit hadn't sounded happy about what she'd heard.

"I was asking Farah for doctor recommendations. She hears stuff, you know."

"So Farah heard something and told you?"

Brigit glanced away. "Would you be offended if I went to a different doctor? I know it's stuff you do every day, but it seems weird...us having grown up together."

"Choosing a doctor is a personal choice." It was easier to distance herself when she was in her office. Here in the coziness of Justin's house, his sister's choice to see someone else stung a little. Logically, she knew that on the patient's end, picking who was going to root around your privates was a deeply personal choice. As a doctor, it was her job. It was clinical.

"I also refuse to see a doctor that spends all of two minutes with each patient like the one you replaced."

That made Priya feel better. "A family practice doctor can provide excellent care."

"I haven't ruled you out yet, but I wanted to let you know that if I go to another doctor, it's only because it's too embarrassing for me to have you see everything. I just want to cover my bases."

Priya couldn't help but give a tiny internal cheer. "Good to hear."

"And that's where my talk with Farah comes in. Some of the people she arrests go on and on about everyone's that done them wrong, or who might do them wrong in the future, and your name was brought up."

"With the women Farah arrests?"

"They said they'd never go to you because you were hired on because of your dad, blah, blah, blah." Brigit rolled her eyes. "Small town. They're going to say that no matter what. But they're also saying that you're not a good doc and you're responsible for Maisy's death."

Cold shock laced down her spine. Her stomach twisted until she wanted to vomit. Suspecting those rumors were being spread was one thing, but to hear that it was real? Tears burned the backs of her eyes.

They were right. The last incident had killed Maisy, but Priya had been her doctor and had suspected she needed medical help. Only she'd been too afraid to urge Maisy to see a therapist, afraid Maisy would stalk off and never talk to her again.

But what if she'd been the only one who could have gotten through to Maisy? She should've done more.

Brigit set Isaiah down on his play mat and leaned forward. "Listen. You're probably wondering why I even told you. Farah asked these women who they do go to."

A hot tear streaked down Priya's face. She swiped it away, but too late. Brigit noticed and hesitated. Priya nodded for her to continue, even though she'd rather run from this humiliating conversation.

"They all see Dr. Bezos."

Priya blinked back the flood of tears waiting to spill. But

these weren't merely from self-pity anymore. It wasn't town gossip scaring her patients away. Everyone wasn't out there wondering if she was so awful at her job that she'd let her friend expire. They were being *told* that. It was targeted rumors, toxic manipulation of her career. Rage licked up her spine. "How many women were there?"

"Maybe like three in the last few weeks." Brigit shrugged. "Enough to make Farah wonder at the source of the rumors."

"Indeed." Dr. Craig Fucking Bezos. It was one thing for her to struggle with her own insecurities, but it was quite another for someone so distanced from the situation, distanced from both her and Maisy, to try and drive her out. "I know he's not my biggest fan, but why? Did he think all his patients were going to abandon him and come to me? Unreal."

But this was all too real. The situation with Maisy had never felt like it was enough to explain her drastic drop in patient load. Yes, it had been an extremely tragic event. But while most people didn't understand medicine, they weren't stupid. Yet if a doctor told them something, they'd believe it.

Like a disease, Dr. Bezos's lies had spread through the clinic's client base and beyond. And because of it, she'd been questioning herself more and more, wondering what she'd done wrong.

Her mind spun.

Male voices drifted through the door. She wiped off her face and took a steadying breath. This was her career. She'd take care of it.

Justin and Caleb piled inside, a cold draft preceding them.

"Did I miss all the fun?" Brigit called, but she eyed Priya to make sure she was okay. Priya's pretend smile grew more confident as her gaze landed on Justin. He always took her mind off the worst.

Brigit stage-whispered across the living room, "I saved all

the work for him. I'm afraid if he doesn't get his hands dirty, I'll come over and he'll be wearing suits and straightening his tie."

An image of Justin in a fitted suit and narrow tie sent flutters through Priya's belly. He was potent enough in the worn jeans and soft plaid flannel he wore now. Pajama pants, no pants, Justin looked good in everything. "I wouldn't mind seeing the suit."

Justin smirked, but quickly looked away as Caleb started speaking. As they walked in and discussed the morning chores with an inquisitive Brigit, Priya ruminated over the news she'd learned.

Bezos was purposely scaring patients off? She had to figure out how to turn him in. It was the only way to deal with the problem, build back trust, and obtain job security.

She could do this.

But how?

As Caleb described the giant huddle of woolly sheep by the barn, Justin laughed. He rubbed his hands together, shot her a look full of *I remember what we did last night*, then turned into a doting dad. Dropping to his knees and crawling across the floor, he played with Isaiah.

She'd have to talk to her dad. She'd have to face looking like less than the competent professional she hoped he saw. But it was the responsible thing to do. And wasn't being a responsible, capable adult the person she strove to be for her parents?

Meeting with Mom and Dad about Dr. Bezos would unlock the next hurdle she'd been preparing to leap. There'd be accusations tossed around. Perhaps an in-house investigation. And at the end either she or Dr. Bezos would be gone.

She was prepared to face reality. Ready for the fight. Willing to look vulnerable and weak and like she didn't have her shit together. Because in the end, she would be ready to move on from this mess.

And she'd be able to face the most difficult confession of all. No more hiding. She'd be ready to tell Justin that she'd fallen in love with him.

CHAPTER 13

The wind had picked up. Gray clouds covered the sky from horizon to horizon. A storm was on its way.

Justin glanced at the clock. Would Priya get here in time? Or would she cancel and not risk being snowed in with him? She had the weekend off.

He hoped she didn't cancel.

Travis and Brigit had just left. Both had stopped by before the bad weather to prepare the sheep as much as possible. They'd checked the shelters, the waterers, and the food supply while he was housebound with a teething baby.

By now, he was used to the help. He bounced Isaiah on his hip. Isaiah was secured with the baby sling and loved everything about walking around with him. Justin was getting used to these contraptions. Even better, Isaiah loved them. The slings would work well in the spring and summer. Justin wouldn't have to rely so much on his family.

But for now, he was housebound and waiting for Priya. A load of laundry waited for him by the recliner and he'd already vacuumed and dusted. He'd rather be outside, but even the inside work was better than sitting in a boardroom all day.

His phone buzzed against the end table. Dammit. Priya was calling to cancel.

He snagged the phone and answered without paying attention to the screen. "Hey," he drawled, infusing as much suggestiveness into his voice as possible. If the roads were bad, he'd tell her not to chance it. But not a flake had fallen yet, and he wanted her to himself.

"Justin Walker. It's been a minute." The feminine giggle on the other end was all too familiar.

His lungs seized until he choked for air. That voice. *She* was on the other end. He'd always had to prepare for her on a good day. Steel himself against her charm and the way she had him dancing before he ever heard a tune.

"Gabrielle." He wrestled Isaiah out of the wrap and laid him on the play mat. Then he walked to the cove of his bedroom as if he didn't want his kid to witness this conversation. "I wasn't expecting you on the other end."

"It sounded like you were." Her breathy tone was there, like it always was. She used it on women and men alike. No matter the gender, they all seemed to succumb to a pretty face saying exactly what they wanted to hear. The meaning behind her words was the kicker.

"I was expecting someone else. What do you need?"

"Can't I just call an old friend? We used to be so close, I can't possibly just cut you out of my life." She could, and she would if it suited her.

"Would your fiancé agree?"

"Percy doesn't babysit me. I can be friends with whomever I please."

Percy was a fellow wolf and was probably using Gabrielle as much as she was using him. With the man's established power and wealth and her tenacity and ambition, they were perfect for each other. Justin didn't want to have anything to do with either of them.

"What did you call for?" This phone call wasn't about small talk. She wanted something from him. He wasn't the naïve twenty-year-old anymore, enamored of the sophisticated coed with big ideas and even bigger opinions.

He also didn't want to fend off any advances, if she dared do that to Percy. It might slip out that he was kind of seeing someone. Gabrielle would sniff out any doubts he had and pounce on them like the predator she was.

He liked the way things were with Priya, and ironically, he had Gabrielle to thank. His ex had ruined him for relationships forever.

"It just so happens I wasn't the only one thinking about you. The VP of Neumen, Fitz, and Ruper is now the CEO. Remember George Nowak? He called the other day, asking about you."

"Send him my best wishes." Landing the NFR account had been his grand finale, the reason Gabrielle had kept him around toward the end. Truthfully, it hadn't been a hardship. George was a nice guy, a family man who wanted the best company for the marketing job, and it'd helped that Justin came from a small ranching community in the Midwest that reminded George of his own hometown in Switzerland.

"He'd love it if you sent them yourself. He arrives in ten days and would love to see you."

And there was the reason she'd called. The first year of the deal he'd secured with George was over and Gabrielle wanted to make sure there were many more happy years of collaboration.

"Pass on my regrets. I can't make it."

"I'd really hate for you to miss out." She peppered her words with a touch of flirty whine. "It hasn't been that long since you've been back to Denver. I'm sure not much has changed."

His hearty laugh ricocheted around the living room. Isaiah started and gave a gummy smile in return. *Not much has changed.* He'd lived a whole other life in the last year.

"I have a kid, Gabrielle."

"Wha—" She was silent so long he wasn't sure she was going to speak again. He relished the shock he'd given her. "I didn't realize—"

"No, you didn't. Because we're through. I don't work with you anymore, and it's not my ring you wear on your finger. I'd love to see George, but you should be glad I'm not going to. I would tell him to find another company whose objectives don't include acting like a chameleon to land big accounts. I would tell him to find a company that isn't run by a sellout."

"Justin, where is this coming from?"

"I'm not doing any work for you anymore. Not as an employee, not as a consultant, and not as a friend. I have a ranch to run and a kid to raise." He almost said son, but he didn't want to give Gabrielle details about his life.

"Are you married?"

He was tempted to answer, but she didn't get more of his time. He was a jean-wearing, scruffy rancher who no longer had to answer to her. "Goodbye, Gabrielle. I mean it. Give George my best, but I'm done with that life." He disconnected.

The expensive watch. A penthouse condo. A cleaning service to scrub away any evidence of his existence in a condo that had never felt homey. Gabrielle's acid-tongued "jokes" about having to reset the clock each time he returned home. He'd been a starched white undershirt away from never visiting his family again.

His visits had started dwindling. That should've been a

giant flag waving that he wasn't comfortable with the guy he was turning into. He used to stop outside of Minnesota on his drive home and change into more casual clothing than his pressed slacks and cashmere sweater. He'd rent a pickup, too.

Pathetic.

He wasn't that guy anymore. The impressionable young kid who'd wanted to prove himself and carve his own place in the world since his older brother had been handed a partnership in the family business. For other people, that life in Denver, the world-traveling businessman, was a perfect fit.

Not him. And he'd been too weak to accept himself.

That was no longer the case. He nudged the basket of laundry aside. It could wait and get wrinkled. He'd wear the clothing, creases and all.

He peeked at Isaiah, then beelined into his bedroom. In the closet, he didn't bother turning on the light. All his old suits hung on one side. Sweeping his arms out and together, he pinched them into one bundle and lifted them off the rack. He dumped them on the ground. When he had time, he'd take the lot to a secondhand store.

He had no need for suits. No one was changing him again.

THE WORDS SPILLED OUT. Once Priya started, she couldn't quit.

She'd entered the sitting room where Dad liked to catch up on the digital version of the *Wall Street Journal* and started talking.

Mom had wandered in halfway through the diatribe, but she'd stayed quiet.

"So, that's where I'm at. What do I do?" She'd been

standing the whole time. Flopping into the padded wicker chair, she ignored the creak. Her mom loved the set and refused to get rid of it.

Priya rubbed her hands on the armrests. Why had she taken so long to approach her parents?

Mom's brow furrowed, and she aimed her gaze at Dad. Shoving a lock of her recently bobbed and freshly dyed chestnut hair behind her ear, she said, "Well, we can't go to the COO. Kirkland and Bezos are golfing buddies."

Kirkland was the clinic's chief organizational officer. Like Bezos, he'd been around forever.

Dad took off his thick-framed readers. The frown that marred his face was what Priya always teased him was his doctor look. "No, definitely not Kirkland. Human Resources. And I'll go with you."

Mom's nod was firm. "So will I."

Priya wanted to cheer, but she had to be realistic. Her parents had a long history at both the clinic and the hospital. They were well respected, but so was Bezos. Priya had heard the rumors about how easily he dispensed pain medication, but she'd never heard of any disciplinary action. Golf buddy and all.

"Won't they cite nepotism if we all march in?"

"True." Mom sighed and leaned back, her chair creaking. "Your father should go with, though. He's had to deal with guys like Bezos his whole career."

Priya turned to her dad. "Really?" She knew his first several years had been rocky, being a city boy in a small town. A new doctor in a tight-knit community. One of the only Indians in a rural Minnesota town. Breaking in and fitting in hadn't been easy, but he'd done it. Even better, he'd stood out.

She hadn't realized the problems continued to happen. He was a popular doctor, and families stayed with him until he treated their kids and even their grandkids. With children, he spoke in whatever accent made them giggle. The top request: pirate. He even dressed the part. Whatever put the kid at ease. Of course, he'd done it all the time for her and Devya.

She should've gone to Dad as soon as her patient load started dropping. His experience would benefit her whether she was his daughter or not. He didn't need to hold her hand, but as a colleague, his advice was invaluable.

"I'll go in first," she said. "Tell me who to talk to and I'll set up a meeting."

"Sarah Mathers has helped me a few times over the years when colleagues or even patients gave me trouble. Don't back down, Pri-Pri." Dad's use of her nickname didn't detract from the grimness of his tone and expression. "There'll always be another Dr. Bezos. Ninety percent of your coworkers will be decent people who only want to help each other, but that ten percent can ruin your career."

Mom reclined in her chair, her chin propped in her hand. "And if you don't clue Human Resources into what's going on, that percentage will crawl far higher than ten percent. Management needs to put a stop to this behavior. We'll do whatever we can to help."

Yes, they would. Wasn't that what they did? With Devya, they cruised in front of her, trying to clear her path. But with Priya, they stood back and waited. Because they cared about her and supported her. They had confidence in her. Maybe she'd only needed some in herself. Confidence that didn't revolve around a grade, or the dean's list.

"Hey, um, I have another scenario to run by you. What would you have done?" As her angst over not urging Maisy to seek mental help spilled out, she marveled over the lack of guilt. They might be her parents, but they were also colleagues and maybe that was the workaround she needed to justify talking about it.

Mom sat forward, the woman who had made known her dislike of Maisy's actions but never forbid Priya from seeing her. "Do you really think it would've changed the outcome?"

How could it not have?

"Say you urged her to get counseling," Dad said. "She would've done one of three things: ignored you, stormed out, or made an appointment. But how long would it have taken her to even make an appointment? How many therapists would she have burned through before finding one that worked for her? And once she reached that level, how long before her behavior changed? Don't forget, she would've had to want it before she picked up the phone to make an appointment. None of it means she would've gone to the doctor for her illness in time. She had an ear infection. Bacterial meningitis is so serious because of how fast it can take a person. How many people would've done exactly what she did and waited it out?"

"The what-ifs kill a career." Mom snuck a glance at Dad. Obviously, they'd been through this conversation before, between themselves. "You made the decision you did at the time for a reason. Have faith in your experience and your education and, in this case, your friendship with Maisy to understand it was the right decision at the time."

She bobbed her head in acknowledgment, but she had no response just yet. Their words were sinking in and needed to marinate. Being alone in her own thoughts had clouded her objectivity.

She was going to Justin's for the night. Around him, her actions in the past made more sense. Orbiting around someone who understood what Maisy was like would help Dad's advice triumph.

She should get going. A storm was coming. Getting

snowed in at home with her parents might be fun, but her desire was to spend the night with Justin. A night both her parents were home, an entire weekend they could spend together and play Monopoly and watch movies, and she was the one opting out.

On Monday, she'd march into Human Resources and file a complaint. By herself.

"Thank you," she said as she rose. "It means a lot. As long as I have you two behind me, I can do this. He isn't going to lie his way into me leaving."

"Don't doubt it. If anyone does, we'll set them straight." Mom's hard tone made her shiver. That was what Priya called her nurse voice. The *don't argue with me* inflection that she used on lazy employees, patients who were refusing treatment to their own detriment, and doctors whose egos got too big for their patients' own good. Mom's next words were softer, infused with curiosity. "Are you going to be gone all weekend again?"

She'd managed to dance around the topic. Her parents were gone so much that she'd honestly wondered if they even noticed. "Probably."

Dad had slipped his reading glasses back on, and he looked at her over the frames. "Surely Justin's baby can't still be having troubles. Are you two seeing each other?"

"N-no. Yes... Not really." Now both parents' laser focus was on her. Somehow, she went from being almost thirty with an advanced degree and a career to a stammering teenager who just wanted to make it out the front door to freedom. "I mean, we're not serious."

Mom's lips thinned. "His decision or yours?"

"Mutual." She shouldn't have to explain more, but the urge was too strong. "With work, I have too much going on."

"And his reason?" Dad wasn't going to let it drop.

"He's not ready to get serious with a baby, so…" *Please drop it. And while you're at it, don't tell anyone.*

Give her this. She didn't do bars. She didn't party. Her old med school friend Natasha had emailed her about a fundraiser in April, a gala to raise funds for a children's hospital. Emmett would be there. She hadn't accepted yet. On the one hand, she wanted to go if only to prove to the world she'd moved on. On the other hand, she wouldn't really be able to prove to *herself* that she'd moved on until she faced Dr. Bezos and had *the talk* with Justin.

Mom and Dad watched her. Bezos and her relationship status would come later, and she wouldn't deal with them at the same time. This weekend was hers. She squared her shoulders. "I won't be home until tomorrow, or Sunday if I get snowed in."

"Okay." Mom managed to say so much with one word. "If you try to drive home and it's snowing, shoot me a message. I'm still going to worry about you on the roads."

She would've made the drive in record time, but she stopped at the grocery store. Justin probably hadn't made a trip in the last week, and in her downtime, she liked preparing meals. He liked eating them.

She grabbed the staples like milk, bread, and butter. Meat wasn't an issue. His basement freezer was stocked with more beef products than the store had on display, and only Justin ate it anyway. Flax and quinoa were the last on her list. She'd promised to make the items that he'd teased her about. *I only touch flax when I'm planting it or harvesting it.*

Challenge accepted.

A few snowflakes landed on her windshield as she drove out to his place. She always looked forward to spending the weekend with Justin. Being on call used to be an obstacle, one that meant she stayed home rather than going to his place, but that hadn't lasted long into the arrangement. The drive to the clinic was farther, but so far it hadn't been a problem.

She parked in her usual spot and grabbed her overnight bag, which held her toothbrush, hair product, soap, a change of clothes, and pajamas. How much of this stuff could be left here for the next time? All of it. But she never did. Maybe this time she could leave her toiletries. He shouldn't balk at that.

Would things change once she had job security again? For her? Probably. What about for Justin?

They'd been doing this for a couple of months now. She didn't want to stop, but how long could she remain the secret lover?

White shit everywhere. Snow drifted over the driveway in piles that probably came up to his chest. Justin stared out the window, squinting in the sun.

It had started snowing late last night, then the wind had picked up this morning. By the afternoon, the clouds had broken apart and the sun now shone. Temperatures were dropping thanks to the clear sky, but the wind had also died down.

"Wow, that's a lot of snow." Priya crossed her arms in front of herself and shivered like just looking at snow dropped her internal temperature a few degrees.

Or it could be the old, drafty picture window.

"I don't think my little skid steer will be enough. When Isaiah naps, I'll go out and clear snow with the tractor."

"You can go now, and I'll watch Isaiah."

He'd been hoping she'd offer, but he was cognizant of not assuming. She wasn't his personal babysitter, and while she truly seemed to enjoy Isaiah, he didn't want her to think that he had her over just for sex and babysitting.

He almost leaned over and grazed a kiss on her forehead. The move would've been so instinctive, the inclination startled him. They fucked. They didn't do things like hold hands or cuddle outside of the bedroom. She had her chair. He had his. Sometimes, she sat on the couch and he hoped it wasn't an unspoken invitation. The longing he had to fold himself around her and snuggle while they watched TV was dangerous. The last thing he wanted was to get rebuffed.

No, the last thing he wanted was to start something beyond what their arrangement was. Yes. That was the last thing he wanted.

He left his pajama bottoms in place and pulled his coveralls on over them. Priya gracefully dropped to the floor to sit next to Isaiah as he chewed on various toys and crinkled them in his little fists. The meal she had going in the Crock-Pot smelled delicious. Vegetarian chili.

The vegetarian dishes she'd made all weekend had him wondering if she was making a statement.

He walked through the kitchen to the back door to find his thick boots and winter gear. The back door was less blocked than the front. He'd use the tractor on what he could, skid steer the smaller areas, and shovel off the rest.

His gaze landed on the bags of groceries she'd picked up. He reminded himself again not to look too hard at it.

This dish soap is easier on my hands.

He bought the same stuff his mom had always used.

Then there was the new bar of soap she'd gotten for the shower. Usually, she packed in and packed out what she brought. But the pale green block smelled faintly of mint and hadn't even come in a box. *It's a natural soap with essential oils. It leaves less gunk in the shower to scrape out. Easier to clean.* Between the two of them, she was the expert about cleanliness, but he couldn't help his mild defensiveness.

Is my shower that bad?

There'd been a nervous tickle in her laugh. *Not at all. But who wants to spend a lot of time cleaning?*

You.

Well...not a lot of time. Scraping soap residue isn't my favorite task.

Yeah, he'd wondered if she'd cleaned his shower a few times.

"Don't worry about the laundry," he shouted from the mudroom as he stepped into his boots. It wasn't a big deal. But after Gabrielle's call he couldn't let it go. She'd started with innocuous stuff, too. First buying an expensive watch when he'd used his phone for all his electronic needs. Then commenting on the neighborhood he'd moved to after leaving the dorms. He should've recognized the behavior after dating Maisy. Her comments about who he hung out with and the way he drove were more than personality quirks. But then, that was the only relationship he'd known.

"It's no problem," she called back.

His jaw tightened. She wasn't an idle woman, but now that he looked, her touch was everywhere. Last night, she'd been in his closet to hang her clothing up so it wouldn't wrinkle in her overnight bag. Did leggings even wrinkle? And she'd hung up the suits he'd dumped in the corner. She'd *oohed* and *awed* over the cut and the labels. *You're just getting rid of them?*

What does a rancher need with a Tom Ford?

She'd laughed and said, *Does one ever* need *a Tom Ford?*

His gaze drifted to the new laundry detergent she'd gotten. He was using one recommended for babies, but she'd gotten a different brand. *The reviews are better.*

Staring at the soft pink label, he leaned out of the mudroom. "You can always come shovel when Isaiah's asleep."

What had made him say that? Had she shoveled before?

Would she even know where to find one? He kept one outside the back door. It had only taken once, wading through thigh-deep drifts to the shed. Now there was always a shovel by the house.

And anyway, she was watching Isaiah so he could push snow. What the fuck had he said that for?

To prove how opposite they were. She was the pampered daughter of a doctor and she would raise equally pampered children. Isaiah already had a tiny little shovel in the barn that was a present from his cousins. As soon as the little guy could walk, he'd be at Justin's boots, helping on the ranch.

He shook his head. That damn phone call had messed him up. He banged out of the house. A knee-high drift started a few feet from the door, but he stomped through it until he reached the shop that held the tractor. Brigit and Caleb had put the snow attachment on last fall for him. It was gassed and ready to go.

The combination of monotony and strategy moving snow required helped distract him from the woman in the house.

Was he going to start being an ass to drive her away? God, he hoped not. She deserved better treatment. They weren't serious, but that didn't mean he didn't respect the hell out of her. So she looked like an astronaut picking her way across Mars whenever she entered the barn. But he probably looked like a duck in the ocean when he walked through the halls of the clinic.

Was that his issue? Did he want more? Was he afraid to want more in case she laughed him off? The grungy rancher and the prim doctor? He birthed lambs and she birthed babies. Same concept, whole worlds apart.

What if she wanted more but only under certain conditions, the main one being that he change?

He was just fine as he was. This life was the one he

wanted. He wasn't here because he was stuck. He was a rancher by choice.

The main driveway was done. He checked the time on his phone. That watch Gabrielle had talked him into years ago had quit working and was stuffed in a drawer somewhere in his house. He needed to give that away, too.

An hour had gone by. The dogs had grown tired of running around the cleared areas and resigned themselves to the barn. He'd spend another hour with the skid steer getting close to the buildings and Priya's car. The road was another story. He lived at a dead-end of sorts. The road split into his drive and the other side was where his cousin Aaron lived. It wasn't an emergency route, and between him and his cousins, they cleared what they could before the county made it this way. Should he start on the road? He had nowhere to go, and there never used to be a reason to rush snow removal. But with Isaiah, he always worried the boy would choke, come down with a freak illness, or—

The freak illness spurred him into action. Not one fleck of snow had been on the ground when Maisy died, but minutes had mattered in her case.

If Priya weren't here, he couldn't even entertain the notion unless he had Isaiah strapped in with him. And how he'd do that, he had no idea.

A red tractor ambled down the drive, blowing a line of snow out of its blower attachment. The arc of white fluff from the blower died as Aaron hit the cleared drive.

Justin's phone rang. Aaron was on the other end. Facing each other like they were going to play chicken, they let the tractors idle.

"Hey," Aaron said as soon as Justin answered. "Just stopping by to see if you needed a hand. The main road is almost clear."

"Thanks, man." Relief pulsed through him. Family saving

his ass was becoming such a regular occurrence that he didn't feel as guilty as he used to. Wasn't that why he'd moved back? They helped each other, and all their work benefitted the company. He wasn't an owner in the company like his brother and four cousins were, but they didn't manipulate him like Gabrielle had. That wasn't always the case with family operations, but he'd grown up with the guys and trusted all of them.

"I see you have some help anyway."

Justin squinted in the direction Aaron was looking. Twisting to look over his shoulder and out of the cab, he spotted Priya. Her puffy white coat blended with the surroundings, but her maroon leggings and knee-high wedge boots stuck out. This pair of boots wasn't suede. They were faux fur lined, but sexy as hell. She had on a knit hat that probably cost as much as the coat, and she was shoveling the sidewalk. The receiver for the baby monitor was hooked to the collar of her coat so she'd hear Isaiah if he woke.

"Fuck me." He hadn't meant to stay that out loud. The guilt sinking into him was at war with the desire that was swiftly rising. She was the sexiest snow bunny he'd ever seen, and he had done plenty of wining and dining at the snow lodges in Colorado.

Aaron's laugh carried over the line. "Maybe I should apologize. She's no longer snowed in with you."

He hoped Aaron could make out his glare. "Thanks for checking on us—me."

More laughter. "If you think you and Priya are a secret, you're not. But no worries, we're keeping it in the family. I don't know why. Daisy's dealt with her in the ER, and she admires the new doc."

Interest cut through his irritation. Aaron's wife—Dalisay to the rest of them, Daisy to Aaron—was a paramedic. He'd thought Brigit was the only one to cross paths with Priya. "Oh yeah?"

"Yep. Dr. Patel treats Daisy like a professional. When that other guy is on call, he's always condescending."

Was that the same guy whose name Priya practically growled? "Dr. B-something?"

"That's the one. I guess the guy has a friend who works in the ER and convinced him to refer patients to him for follow-up."

"So Priya gets fewer follow-up patients."

"Daisy said there was a reason there was an OB opening. The last lady couldn't take the bullshit and left."

What was Priya going to do?

He didn't have a chance to reply when Aaron broke in. "But I'm sure you've heard all about it. I'll leave so you can help your girlfriend. She's not getting anywhere fast."

Aaron's tractor started beeping as he backed out of the drive. Justin looked over his shoulder again. Priya was watching the other tractor. He could see where she'd shoveled, and Aaron was right. It'd take her an hour to get off the landing. She spotted him staring at her and waved.

He couldn't help his smile as she went back to tackling the drift. She was shaving inches off the top, working her way down to the cement. She might not have the upper body strength to throw full shovel loads of wet snow, but she used that sharp mind of hers to tackle the problem.

But then her intellect was never the problem. His was being smart enough not to fall for her.

Justin hadn't stopped to chat when he switched tractors. Now he was cruising around in a Bobcat and arranging piles of snow she thought were already out of the way. For a guy who left his pants on the floor wherever they landed, he was particular about the outside of the house.

The shop doors were open, and nothing was parked haphazardly. She couldn't name all the equipment inside, but each one had its spot. The big green contraption Justin used for the bulk of the snow was parked outside for now, giving her a view into rancher Justin.

The barn was dirty. Dirt floor, straw, and manure, but beyond all that, the stalls were ordered. Gates didn't hang off hinges and equipment didn't litter the floor.

He took pride in his work. In his home? Not so much.

Her life was the opposite. During surgery, she had nurses and surgical techs who cleaned up after her. Environmental staff wiped, dusted, and mopped. After each appointment, the nurse or CNA readied each room. She went to work and could leave a trail behind her that others were literally trained to clean up. She didn't, but she could. At home, she bordered on militant about every item having its spot.

Both areas of her life were all about order and cleanliness. Maybe what she needed was an outlet, one other than baking. It might need to be a hobby that satisfied her craving for order—or one that burned that need for order to cinders.

How she was going to make order out of this snow, she didn't know, but she wanted to be productive. When he'd come out to move snow, he'd seemed cranky—perhaps it was the magnitude of the storm in addition to all the normal work he struggled to attend to that had him in a mood. If that wasn't it… Was *she* annoying him? So she'd folded, done dishes, and packed most of her items. She'd only wanted to help out.

With Justin's tracks busting through the compact drifts, she could hack away at the looser areas around his footprints. Hack away with the muscles she didn't have.

Sports hadn't been her thing in school. She'd been buried

in books, earning those As, and gathering volunteer hours at the clinic for the honor society. There'd been nothing about the sports life she missed until now.

Stuffing the shovel into the snowbank, she heaved upward. Too much. She yanked out the shovel and picked another spot that would pile less snow on. No wonder heart attacks were so prevalent after a person shoveled a driveway. She was weak as hell.

Sweat dotted her brow, frosting across the material of her hat. Her arms burned, but exhilaration flooded through her. Fresh air, hard work, and the short path she'd already cleared gave her a sense of accomplishment. Lifting weights might have to replace her cleaning time as an outlet for stress relief.

She was breathing hard and sweat soaked through her shirt. They'd go into the wash immediately. She hadn't turned over that big of a leaf.

Snow crunched behind her. So zoned into her work, she hadn't noticed that Justin was done with the Bobcat. She stabbed the shovel into the pile she'd built up at the edge of the sidewalk and turned around.

How could the man be covered from head to toe and still have that sexy swagger? Breath puffed around him as he stalked toward her. "You don't have to be out here."

Had snow removal only made him more irritable? "I wanted to help, not sit around while you were doing all the work."

He wiped snow crystals off his beard and let out a breath, his shoulders falling. "You made good progress. Let me know if you find a Leatherman. I lost one during our first snowfall. I keep reaching for it when I'm out here tinkering around, but I might have to wait for spring."

She surveyed behind her. The clearing was barely two feet wide, but she'd made it down the stairs and another six feet. "I've been out here an hour. I don't think my progress is that good." But what little she'd done had pleased him. Much better than sitting on her ass, scrolling through channels.

"Be honest. Have you ever shoveled?"

"Um…" Her first inclination was to say no. But, dang it, she'd been born and raised in Minnesota, how could she not have shoveled before? So her dad cleared what he needed to before work and the snow removal person he hired had the job done before she and Devya left for school in the morning. "I'm sure Devya and I played in the snow. With a shovel?"

He laughed, the sound getting carried away on the wind. "Are you asking or telling?" He came closer, his overalls whistling together. "You didn't have to come out here. I was joking."

It hadn't felt like it. She cooked and she cleaned, and while he didn't take her for granted, the competitive part of her had to prove that she could do more. He didn't think she could clear snow, so she cleared some damn snow. Not much, but she'd done it.

She evaluated the path she'd cut. "I'm actually taking a liking to it."

His brows rose to the bottom of his hat. "Dr. Patel is going to take a side gig?"

"No. Maybe a hobby of moving my body." She smiled, and it came out flirtier than she'd intended. Had to be from the endorphins of her recent physical activity. "This got me thinking."

"Moving snow gives you plenty of time to do that."

"I don't have anything but work." She didn't say that she had him. Because she didn't. And if she did, that wouldn't be healthy. A family being the center of her world was one thing, but not just a guy.

If there was one thing being friends with Maisy had made clear, it was that she needed to broaden her circle of friends.

Aside from Maisy's darker personality traits, Maisy's mess had been allowed to flourish because of a lack of social support. Priya had been glued to Maisy's side out of fear of being rejected by others. Always teased for her intense study habits and her single-minded pursuit of her chosen career, she'd stayed friends with Maisy because it was safer. They had each complemented the others' insecurities. She'd needed a friend who just let her be and didn't push her outside of her comfort zone, and Maisy had needed to feel superior in some way. Socially awkward and meek Priya had done that for her.

"What do you want to do?" he asked.

"Maybe join a gym, go to some classes."

"More school?" He wasn't asking as a criticism. A small detail, but an important one to her.

"No, nothing with homework. I'm over those years." And she was. She'd gone to college and submersed herself in studying, and she'd even found a like-minded group that she was still in contact with. But they'd all moved on. Emmett certainly had. It was time for her to do so, too.

"I know what you mean."

Despite the warmth his support infused her with, she shivered. She'd worked up a sweat and had quit moving.

He ushered her through the door, leaving the shovel sticking up in the snowbank. "Tell me more about going out as we go in."

Crowding into the house, the heat of the mudroom washed over her, but she was still chilly. She stepped out of her boots. Her frigid toes sank into the rug, bits of snow they'd tracked in melting into her socks. Another shiver racked her body. Yeah, she needed better boots.

"You need to get out of that wet stuff." He unzipped her coat even though he had to be roasting in his heavy coveralls. The mix of fresh snowy air and exhaust from the tractor clung to him. It shouldn't be appealing, but it was. It shouldn't be fueling the bloom of heat kindling inside of her belly, but it was.

"Ugh, I'm all sweaty. You don't have—"

"None of that bothers me, not after I watched a little snow bunny muscle her way through drifts half her height." He plucked the monitor off her collar and set it on the bench that ran along the wall.

Her chill was retreating against the heated look in his eye. "This snow bunny isn't sure what to do about a big mountain man looking like he wants to devour her."

A blond brow lifted, and he ripped his hat off. Locks of his hair stuck out and the rest was plastered to his scalp. "Mountain man?" He shed his coveralls and boots. Static cling and his own perspiration molded his shirt to his body. That body. He was a wall of man in front of her. She was too busy ogling his muscles to react when he moved.

A shriek caught in her throat as he rubbed his whiskered chin along her neck. Only the thought of waking Isaiah stopped her from yelling, and not even her aversion to dirty, messy surroundings could stop the bonfire of desire Justin started just by…being him. She wiggled, but he banded his arms around her like a vise, not squeezing, but the bunny was trapped.

"I'm not shaving," he growled into her neck as she writhed in his arms.

She wasn't asking him to. "If you keep being naughty with that thing," she gasped as he nuzzled her again, "I might shave it in your sleep."

His strong arms gripped her under her ass and lifted. "Try it, and I'll put dirty sheets on the bed before you come next time."

"Gross!" She dissolved in laughter as he carried her to his bathroom. He quit teasing her with his beard, but she took over, tangling her hands in his hair and tightening her legs around him.

By the time he deposited her next to his shower and closed the door, she didn't feel the cold. He peeled his shirt off as he stalked toward her. She did the same, tossing it where he'd dropped his. They watched each other as they undressed. It was their own private, hurried strip show.

He maintained eye contact as he opened a drawer in the vanity next to him and withdrew a condom packet. She flipped the shower lever to a setting that'd warm them both —not that they'd need it.

He advanced on her, bringing to life a fantasy she hadn't known she had about being snowed into a cabin in the mountains with a reclusive beast of a man. Normally she would've jumped in and washed off before he touched her. But now she was under his spell.

He had enough foresight to test the spray of water before drawing them both inside and closing the door behind him. "I'm impressed," he murmured as he backed her against the cool tile. Warm spray pelted the side of her body. He moved enough to let the water hit her and heat her body and the wall behind her, but he was still pressed against her, his erection throbbing between them. "I didn't think you'd let me get this far." He skimmed his hand down her belly and slicked his fingers through her folds.

Her moan was amplified in the stall. She widened her stance and twined her arms around his neck. "You're hard to resist."

In one smooth move, he lifted her and angled his shaft to slide inside as she settled on him. The way he filled her so completely chased away the rest of the cold. They were moving. Or he was, and she gave herself over to his thrusts. Her breasts rubbed against his chest, heightening the sensations of the water hitting her fevered skin, the stroke of him inside her, and the hard wall pinning her to his solid chest.

Her entire body tightened. She clung to him. Their lips met and opened immediately. Wet tongues clashed as their bodies worked in harmony to reach a mutual peak. His shoulders were rigid, his legs braced. He was close. She strained against him, the tease of her clit as they smashed together not quite enough to push her over the edge.

She almost shouted in relief when he wedged an arm between them, not stopping until his fingers grazed her nub. She melted against him, her moans and whimpers mixing with his grunts as his hips flexed harder and faster.

She couldn't call his name or shout yes as she peaked. They were too tied together. Their mouths fused, joined at the sex, her legs anchoring her to him. Careening over the summit, she came hard. A long groan resonated from him into her, like a human-sized vibrator sending little waves through her nipples and her belly. His strokes shortened until he stiffened with his release. She rode out hers as he climaxed.

Their kiss went from frantic and needy to slow until they finally broke apart. "You're welcome to come shovel anytime."

"You might've created a monster." If this was how it ended, she'd be over here for every snowfall.

His smile was as hot as the look in his eyes. He might not have been done if it wasn't the middle of the afternoon and she had to get home. He didn't leave the shower like she'd expected, only leaning out to dispose of the condom.

She took the soap she'd bought for him, hoping he didn't mind her suggestion. He didn't seem like the body-wash type, so she'd stuck with bar soap that wouldn't gross up the shower. Lathering up the brick in her hands, she washed his chest down first. He snatched it from her and worked it until suds covered his big hands. Then she was next.

He dipped his hands lower until a shudder ran through her from head to toe. Were they going to do it again? She had to get home and prepare for the week, and Isaiah could wake any minute.

"Just to show you what will be waiting for you next time." He washed her down completely, his touch gentle but full of suggestion.

"I don't think I'm at risk of forgetting." She might not be able to wait until next weekend.

Once they were all dried off, she went to the mudroom to grab her coat and boots. The front door would be easier to get out. The stairs weren't cleared yet, but it was a shorter span before she reached the cleared-off drive. And her packed bag was there.

She carried her things through the kitchen. Justin was waiting at the front door next to her purple bag. His hands were full of her toiletries. Toothbrush. Toothpaste. Hair product.

"I didn't want you to forget these."

Out of the goodness of his heart? Or because he had to maintain such a strict line of friends with benefits that she couldn't even keep a toothbrush here? "Oh, okay. Thanks."

She opened her bag, grabbed them from his hands, and dumped them inside. Uncharacteristic of her. What if they spilled, oozed, or smeared residue over her clothing? She didn't care. The hurt burning inside of her cleared out her need for order.

"Give Isaiah a kiss for me when he wakes." She heaved the bag over her shoulder and darted outside.

"Wait."

Would he apologize? Was this the moment they'd have the talk? The one where they moved ahead into the real relationship she couldn't deny she wanted? The only other direction was backward, and she didn't know if she could be just friends as he forged ahead in life—with someone else.

"Let me shovel the steps before you—"

"It's not bad." Cleaning off the snow was a sweet gesture but not the topic she'd both hoped and feared he'd bring up. The need to leave overwhelmed her. She charged down the steps, didn't slip, and scurried to her car.

Oh, hell. She'd have a pile of snow on her car.

No. She almost pulled up short. All the snow was brushed off and the windows had even been scraped.

That was it. When he did kind, thoughtful gestures like this, her hopes rose. She wanted more. She wanted his actions to mean more. But he'd probably do the same for his sister. For Caleb. For any other person he called friend. A word that was no longer good enough for her.

CHAPTER 15

The morning was another brisk one. Priya was grateful to be inside while Justin was out doing chores. Her snow-moving experience during the last storm had proved that she wasn't cut out for ranching life. Her body had ached for days.

But it had propelled her toward a gym membership. Spin class each morning gave her the serenity to face passing Dr. Bezos in the halls as Human Resources researched her claims. She grinned and beared her way through the dirty glares from his nursing staff and his pompous grunts each time he passed her office.

Each weekend, she woke up with Justin and refused to think about work. Until last week, when Sarah from HR had called her and said that Dr. Bezos was being encouraged to retire—or he'd be fired.

Her job was secure, and she'd passed through the drama —with her parents' help, but without her hand being held. Her insecurities had died down in time with the turmoil at work. Perfect timing. Today was Valentine's Day. She was ready for a real relationship and she only wanted one with

Justin. Her gaze strayed to her overnight bag. She had a little gift for him.

The day was all planned out. Make pancakes for breakfast —regular round pancakes, not heart-shaped ones. They'd eat, and she'd present him with her gift, an engraved Leatherman multitool, and broach the subject of dating for real.

This would work. She washed up, brushed out her hair, and loosely tied it back. She'd release it after she cooked. The way Justin ran his hands through it and buried his face in her tresses—well, anything helped.

Isaiah's cry came over the monitor. She went upstairs and into the nursery. "Good morning, little guy," she cooed. He was such a happy baby. He grinned and wiggled as she picked him up.

She didn't get to see babies much after she brought them into the world, but moms sometimes had them with during their follow-ups. The visits were quick and she cherished them, but other than helping them be born, and perhaps being their OB/GYN in the future, her role in their life was minimal. Being a part of Isaiah's life was a gift, and not just because he connected her to the best parts of her lost friend.

She knew his cries, she witnessed his smiles, and she even made him giggle. Every time she was in the store, she found cute new clothes, bibs, and toys. Last night, she'd wrapped him in a new fluffy blanket with duckies on it after his bath.

And these morning cuddles with Isaiah while she fed him his bottle were the highlights of her days. Once he was done, she started on breakfast. The tiny package was wrapped and tucked away in the silverware drawer. She already had the small kitchen table set for just the two of them.

As she was alternating between scrambling eggs and flipping pancakes, the back door opened, and Justin stomped inside, banging the snow off his boots.

"Smells good." The deep growl of his voice sent delicious

shivers through her. If all went well today, maybe during nap time she'd get to experience those naughty whiskers of his up close and personal—again.

"Pancakes and eggs."

"My favorite."

He said that about everything she made. While she suspected it was his gimmick, she'd tested it earlier when she made her dad's creation—vegetarian chili. And no cornbread. She'd used her Nana's recipe for pav buns instead.

But no, her rancher and diehard meat lover had cleaned up two bowls of chili and half a dozen buns.

She finished up at the stove. Bringing the food to the table as he washed up in the mudroom, her hands shook only slightly. She hadn't been this nervous since taking her board exams.

Justin came around the corner, rubbing his hands. "I'm famished." He popped out to the living room to drop a kiss on Isaiah's head before he came back. "Can I help with anything?"

"Nope. Sit."

Playing it cool through the whole meal taxed her limited acting skills. She finished before him. To keep from fidgeting at the table, she cleared her plate.

After placing her dishes by the sink, she ran her finger over the counter.

"Found something to clean again?" Justin shoveled another forkful of eggs in his mouth.

"No, it's not that. Whenever I'm here, I always imagine how this room would look after a remodel."

His chewing slowed, and he looked around. When he turned his gaze back on her, his eyes were a few shades darker.

Had she upset him? "It's just that this L cuts off flow. An island, maybe." She walked forward a few steps and held her arms out. "Right here. Oh, and the cupboards. They go all the way to the ceiling, which works for you. I'm too short for the top shelves. But if you opened up the top— And that wall." She was babbling now as she pointed at the wall bordering the dining room. "I know it's supporting, but even a cutout? This kitchen feels like a dungeon."

He sawed his fork over more pancakes, his jaw clenched. "It worked for my parents for a few decades."

"And I'm sure your parents have a more spacious kitchen in their new house." She pressed her lips together. That might've gone too far. But she bet if Justin's parents could build this house over again, they'd plan a different layout.

"Well, it's just me here." He played it off like it was no big deal. Was he wary because she was proposing changes to his beloved childhood home, or because she was doing so while only maintaining friendship status?

Maybe it was the wrong time, or the best moment ever. She crossed to the drawer she hid his present in and withdrew it. "I got you a little something."

When she turned to face him, she wished she could take her words back and stuff the box into a dark corner. His expression was carefully neutral, his gaze cautious.

"It's Valentine's Day." Her explanation hung heavy between them. The box made the only sound in the room as she put it on the table next to him.

"Okay." He carefully placed his fork next to his plate and leaned back. "But we're just friends."

"That's what I wanted to talk to you about. When we first started…being together—"

"Having sex. You're a doctor, remember."

Any nerves she had were wiped out by hurt, but she wasn't backing down. She had a right to say how she felt, to express herself. The last few weeks, she'd worked on herself and her career. Continuing on with Justin, feeling the way she did about him, wasn't fair to her. However this ended, it wouldn't be with her selling herself short.

"When we first started having sex"—she held his gaze—"I was facing job insecurity and my own little personal identity crisis."

"Really? See, I didn't know that. Since you never talked to me about it when it was happening."

"I wasn't sure about what was going on at work until a few weeks ago. Then when I was here, I didn't want to stew over how I was treated." Maybe admitting that her career was tanking had felt a little too intimate for her. She shook her head and attempted to steer the conversation back to her goal. No matter how this turned out, he'd know how she felt. "All I'm saying is that I'm in a different place now. I'm ready for more."

THIS CONVERSATION WAS REALLY HAPPENING. Justin shoved a hand through his hair. He didn't want to experience it now—or ever. What they had was good. It had been going well. But this morning as she was telling him she was ready for more, she was redesigning the cupboards—the whole kitchen.

She watched him. Her lips were flat, like the look in her eyes. No, her golden eyes weren't emotionless. They swirled and heaved with repressed feelings. If he thought too hard about it, he'd recall they'd been that way forever. She always hid what she was really thinking.

"What do you want from me?" he finally asked.

"A real relationship." She was so frustratingly calm, so centered when she'd just left him feeling as shaky as a newborn lamb.

She was ready for more. And happened to be ready to change the way he lived. No, thanks. Been there. Done that.

He wasn't changing a damn thing. The house fit him the way it was. The way *he* was, and he didn't fucking cook. "I told you that I'm not in it for a relationship."

Hurt brimmed in the depths of her irises. "Can you really say that after the last few months? That we wouldn't work as a couple?"

"The level of trustworthiness of the women in my life hasn't made me think that couplehood is for me."

She recoiled and gave him an incredulous stare. "What have I lied about?"

"Come on, Priya. You don't talk to me about anything. You don't talk to me about your family, or about the problems you have at work."

"I recall us having several conversations about that."

"You mention it. Skim the surface. Not once did you really confide in me. I found out from a nurse at Gram's nursing home that you were alone on Thanksgiving. What's that supposed to make me think? I told you my history with Gabrielle. You know what Maisy was like. Maybe you didn't lie, but you weren't open and honest." Months of wanting her to share more about herself rose. His own hurt at being sidelined in her life lifted with it.

"How much would you have told me about Maisy if I hadn't been her friend? As for your previous career and that other woman, you talked for less than five minutes about how many years of your life? And you think *I* don't share about myself?"

"If you wanted to know more, then you could've asked."

"I did. How many nights did we sit out there while you waved off my every attempt to open a conversation?" She tilted her head.

So many hours they'd spent over a glass of wine while apparently pondering how little they talked to each other about each other. "You mean like you did every time I tried to ask about work?"

Isaiah let out a happy squeal in his swing, oblivious to the tension radiating only feet away.

"I would think you of all people would understand my hesitation when it comes to sharing any part of my life. Maisy changed my entire life with one impulsive decision."

Priya's gaze lifted to where Isaiah was, as if talking about Maisy around her baby boy was inappropriate. And yeah, maybe it was. Justin would have to reconcile how he was going to talk about Isaiah's mother around him with his feelings for the woman.

Priya had mentioned the discussion in his bathroom where he'd laid out his humiliation over Gabrielle. He recalled another part of that talk that continued to bug him. "And while we're on the topic, tell me the truth. Was Isaiah really an accident?" The way her mouth gaped like a guppy caught on shore sent the most acute spike of betrayal into his heart. "You knew?"

"No." She shook her head, but her gaze flew around the room. "Not until after you two— She wasn't on the pill."

"She lied? *You* lied?"

"She was my patient. She told me during the very first appointment after the condom broke that it was an old condom." Her shoulders hunched, and she mumbled, "A really old condom."

"Did she also tell you that she told me she was on birth control and not to worry about it? And I didn't, and we kept —" He snapped his mouth shut. He was so stupid. "*You knew.*"

"What would telling you have done?"

She waited for an answer but he didn't have one. What would he have done?

"Maybe it's time you quit hiding behind Maisy and how she treated us." She did *not* just say that. "You're using her to justify sleeping with me without accepting any responsibility for how you treat me."

"That's rich," he scoffed. "You were the one who was afraid being linked to me would be bad for your career."

"How do you think it would've turned out for me, after they were being told that I was responsible for Maisy's death?"

"It's a good thing you looked out for yourself."

Her hands fisted by her sides and her eyes flashed fire. "Do you know how long I've liked you, Justin Walker? Since before she got her hooks in you. But you went willingly. You strung her along as much as she did you, and all the while I played the supportive, happy friend. Years later, I'm still doing it. You're right. You know what's changed? I have. I have a loving and supportive family and a career I worked hard and fought for, and I'm ready for a real relationship. If you weren't so concerned about shying away from expectations, using every woman who wronged you as an excuse, then maybe you'd see how well we worked."

It took a few moments for her words to sink in. She'd liked him as more than a friend for… He'd been fifteen when he'd started dating Maisy. Neither she nor Priya had ever mentioned it. Priya had never hit on him. Never sent glances his way full of invitation.

She didn't wait for him to respond. "I deserve to be more than a sidepiece. I deserve the trust of my partner. I deserve more."

More wasn't part of their deal. "You agreed to this arrangement."

"Until now." She folded her arms. In the mix of his tangled emotions, he still noticed how nicely the move shoved her bust up. The curtain of her hair shaded half of her face, highlighting the sad shadows in her expression. "I'm not going to beg. I did that once before, but I'm not going to let a man blame me for his own insecurities."

"Sounds like another story you didn't tell me about."

"No, I didn't. Here's the story: He got into a prestigious fellowship and decided I was too tedious and boring to keep seeing. I cried. I begged. Then I ran home and moved in with my parents. See? You're not the only with past relationship issues."

"Which is why I don't want another one." The words tasted bitter as he said them. He didn't. Did he?

Her expression went stony. "I see. I guess I have my answer."

Yes.

No.

Wait. What did he want?

She stormed toward the foyer. Priya's announcement, Maisy telling him she was pregnant, and the moment he'd found out Gabrielle's fiancé had bought his company rotated in his head on a hamster wheel. "You liked me in high school and never mentioned anything."

"Oh, I mentioned something, just not to you. Why else do you think Maisy hit on you so hard?"

He reeled back a step. The relationship that had started his mess of a personal life had been a calculated move to hurt Priya? "And you knew about that?"

She let out a puff of impatience. "Yes, Justin. You got me. Another woman hiding how awful someone was to you when it was all right there in front of your face."

She gathered her purse and put on her shoes. From his spot at the table, he didn't miss the longing look she shot Isaiah before digging out her keys.

"I was a teenager." Dammit, he couldn't let it drop. Too many revelations, all on top of Priya vacating his life.

The expression she directed at him said he should know

better. "Not when you came back to town, turned down Maisy's advances, then suddenly hooked up with her one night, igniting all the hopes she'd clung to since graduation. Who's the bad guy in that scenario? Her actions afterward were all on her, but don't forget you were the one who arrived on her doorstep to use her for your own reasons."

He worked his jaw. The accuracy of her shot burned. He'd turned to Maisy out of spite. "She shouldn't have—"

Priya cut a hand in the air. "Instead of blaming everyone around you when your life doesn't go the way you want it to, maybe start with yourself first." She slammed out the door, the sound echoing through the house.

Isaiah's happy babbles died down as he chewed on a fist. His eyes were full of alarm and he was on the verge of tears.

Justin let out a slow breath. It was probably the same expression he wore. He trudged over to Isaiah and sank into the recliner next to the swing. "It's all right, kiddo. We'll be all right."

There was no conviction in his voice. As he stared out the picture window, Priya drove away, and he didn't move. This was the chair he sat in when they spent their evenings together. He'd had more fun here than in any bar.

The dishes were waiting in the kitchen. He would do them and recall their happy conversation over breakfast and her giggles of anticipation as she prepared to jump him with her questions about their future.

The stupid gift. He'd never opened it.

With a heavy sigh, he heaved out of his chair. Isaiah batted at his toys on his swing's mobile. Justin would clean up the kitchen and spend the afternoon playing with the boy until nap time.

The gift sat on the table, mocking him.

Glowering down at it, a million questions ran through his head. Why had she gotten him something? Why couldn't she be satisfied with the way things were? Why did she have to tell him that she'd liked him since they'd been kids? Why did she suddenly have to become all stubborn and walk out on him?

He flipped the top off the rectangular box. Air escaped his lungs like a horse had kicked him in the gut. "Fuck me."

A black pouch that would fit on his belt rested inside. He knew exactly what was inside. Touching the pouch like it was a thousand degrees, he dumped out the Leatherman tool.

It was engraved with his initials and a note in her scrawling, barely legible doctor's handwriting that said, *Don't worry if you lose it, I'll have another made.*

She'd remembered he'd lost his other one and guessed he'd probably lose this one, too. But it was more important he get use out of it than...some expensive watch he didn't need.

He slumped into his chair in the kitchen and buried his head in his hands. The reality that he'd destroyed a future relationship with Priya was sinking in. Worse, the friendship he'd been so worried about tarnishing had been annihilated.

CHAPTER 16

Claudia, the clinic administrator, clasped her hands on her desk. "I can't apologize enough, Dr. Patel. Dr. Bezos's behavior toward you was inexcusable and, well, we know how it turned out for the former COO."

Right. There were two new openings in the clinic. "I wish I hadn't waited so long to lodge a complaint."

Her boss's forehead creased. "That's never something I want to hear. Rest assured, we're combing through the process and removing any trouble. Prescription abuse alone is a serious issue, and the rest could cost us valuable employees and, even worse, patient trust."

"Thank you. So much."

Claudia moved like she was going to get up, but hesitated. "I hope you realize that you were hired based on your resume and letters of recommendation. That fact that Dr. Patel is your dad was more of an obstacle for you, for the very reason you're in my office."

Nepotism. "I understand. But it's good to hear." It was fabulous to hear. She hadn't been hired because of her dad. Fuck Bezos and his rumors.

Two weeks had passed since she'd walked out of Justin's. Her career was secure. She'd never been more open with her parents. She should be floating out of the office, but her feet were as heavy as lead. Or those thick steel-toed boots Justin wore when he moved snow. They'd made her wedge boots look so small and delicate.

Like, a rancher's wife?

Why not? So she didn't travel to exciting places like Devya for work or help birth lambs in the middle of a pasture like Justin. Yes, her work environment was more controlled, but she still occasionally found herself on a stool with both hands inside of a woman, pulling a tiny human out. Okay, so the stool part didn't happen often, but even some C-sections required more leverage, different positions, and were messy in their own right. Very messy. And smelly. She couldn't hold up her hands and declare that she wasn't cut out for the job.

He didn't want a relationship, not even one with her. Maybe she could've done things differently to change his mind, but…he could've, too. She missed Isaiah. She'd shed tears over both of them.

After leaving Claudia's office, she stepped outside and burrowed her chin into her collar. The March wind had a hint of warmth to come, but it was still cold this time of year. No trees had begun budding, and everything was still brown.

Cold and dead.

Sort of how she felt inside.

She glanced at the time. She had the afternoon off since she'd been on call earlier in the week. What to do?

Her phone was in her hand before she gave it much thought. The number was dialed. Her non-relationship with Justin had been terminated, but there was another she'd neglected for too long.

This time when Devya answered, there was no music banging on the other end. *"Bonjour?"*

"It's me."

"Good. I can speak English and not pretend I'm British."

A laugh escaped Priya. "Why would you do that?" Though Dev was probably excellent at it. All she had to do was copy Papa and Nana.

"Artists can be…weird. I get more street cred as British than I do as American. People here see how I look and don't know what to say when an American accent comes out. Especially if my Minnesotan slips and I say uffda."

"Some of the patients are still like that," she said drily.

"Seriously?" Her frustrated sigh gusted over the line. "Anyway, what's up?"

"I called to see how you're doing."

The other end of the line went quiet. "Are Mom and Dad worried?"

"I'm worried. We need to talk. Do you want to go first, or do you want me to?" She wasn't giving Devya an option to back out. They were sisters. They were going to talk like sisters.

"You? I've gotta hear this."

"Only if you promise to tell me what's going on with you."

"Cross my heart."

"Remember when I mentioned hanging out with Justin Walker?" The story poured out of her like floodwaters over sandbags.

"Pri…" Devya breathed. "I don't know whether to be sad or proud. I'm a little of both, actually. And mad at him. What the fuck is he thinking? He'd be lucky to have you."

She should've called Devya weeks ago. "I wish I could sound as righteous, but you were right. He grows wool, I prefer cashmere."

"Then wear cashmere! *On s'en fout.*"

"You know I don't speak French."

"I said 'who cares.' But you deserve the best and if he doesn't see it, then he's not the best."

Her head knew it was true, but her heart refused to get the message. "Don't think I forgot our deal. Talk."

Priya started the car to kick in some heat. Laying her head back and closing her eyes, she listened as Devya described her perceived failures as an artist and her refusal to come back until she made something of herself. Turned out that having two highly professional and driven parents and a sister who followed in the same footsteps was intimidating. Devya was hindered by insecurity. Enough so that it affected her daily routine until she neglected her responsibilities and partied instead.

She stared at the cloudy sky. "That's why our parents and grandparents are worried about you."

"I'm proof it's possible to babysit someone from thousands of miles away."

"I've always been jealous of you, you know."

"You're kidding."

She wished. "Serious as a heart attack."

"Dad always says that."

"I know. Being the responsible one means it feels like you get all the attention. Ask me if it still bothers me even though we're adults."

"*I* get all the attention? They call me and talk about *you*. Priya did this. Priya did that. They're so proud of you."

Hadn't this argument been part of Justin's issues with her? She didn't talk. Not about herself, and never about her life. She'd been doing it to her sister, too. "They're proud of you, too. You have talent and you're chasing it. Don't give up. Unless it's driving you crazy. Then come home."

Devya chuckled. "Is that your professional opinion?"

"Yes. And I miss your face." An idea popped into her head,

and it sounded better and better the more she thought about. "I'm going to come visit you."

Devya let out a delighted gasp. "When? I have a break in classes this summer."

"Send me the dates. There's no better way to use my vacation time."

"Uh-huh. And if the hot sheep farmer finds his brains by then, bring him, too."

The sadness she'd been trying to fight off rushed back. "It'll just be me."

"Mm-hmm. Either way, come see me. Just give me warning so I can clean before you get here. I made a deal with myself to not return until I can afford my own ticket back."

"Then I'll come out and visit as often as I can." And she'd be by herself.

"You're not going home all sad now, are you? I can't let you do that."

"You're half a world away."

"Convince me you're going to do something for yourself."

Devya and her "do something for yourself." How often had she been right and Priya had been annoyed? "There's this party. A fancy one."

"Tell me more."

Priya explained about Natasha, her ex, and the gala. "I was hoping I could go show Emmett what he'd missed, but I'm not feeling it."

"One, he did miss out. Two, fake it until you make it."

"Fine. I'll go." She'd go and live out the moment she'd fantasized about. Emmett would see the new Priya, the one who'd fought for her job and won. He didn't have to know she'd fought for her man and lost.

But before she did anything for herself, she had a call to make. The sudden decision was too important for her to chicken out. She'd put it off so long, and because of it, the whole town had fallen for Dr. Bezos's bullshit.

Okay, not the whole town. But enough that she had some spin control to do.

When Katherine answered, Priya jumped in. "Hi. It's Priya. Can you meet me for a drink?"

THE LOUD MUSIC irritated every last nerve, but it was better than the quiet at home. Isaiah made his share of noise, but he wasn't the best conversationalist yet. And he was staying the night with his grandparents.

After sitting in his house for an hour with a glass of wine he hadn't touched, he'd called Caleb. It was April and he'd thought the lambing season would take his mind off how badly he missed Priya. No. He was tired and cranky. Every morning this week, Brigit and Caleb had played paper-rock-scissors in front of him to decide who got to hang out inside with Isaiah and who had to deal with his crabby ass.

He shouldn't run them off. Most days, they were the only adult interaction he got. Not that he wanted to talk to anyone else. He only wanted to talk to one person, but she hadn't even texted since she'd left.

And if she had, what would he have said? *I don't care if you talk to me or not, just come back?*

Not talking hadn't worked out well last time.

Justin nursed his beer. Caleb was across from him, and he had just waved Lucas over. Lucas was a couple years older than them, but since he used to pal around with Aaron, who was married with kids now, Lucas palled around with anyone who'd have him.

Lucas set his foamy mug on the table and sat down. Looking at Caleb, he asked, "Bridge let you out of the house?"

Justin could answer for him. Brigit had probably told Caleb to try and cheer her brother up, or talk some sense into him. His sister bugged him at least once a week. *Have you called her yet?*

Why would I call her?

Because, as my brother, you get away with not saying much. You can't do that with someone you care about.

He'd asked why she assumed it was him and not just her.

I'm your twin *and you barely talk to me.*

Since when had she become Priya's number-one fan?

"She's at an ag convention with Farah all weekend." Caleb pushed his empty bottle to the edge of the table.

"I should've gone to that one, too." Lucas took a swig, his gaze roaming the bar. Whenever he was in here, he always seemed distracted. Was that his normal? Or did he come here for someone?

Thinking about it took Justin's mind off Priya. Oh look. He was back.

Katherine mentioned that they'd met for lunch last weekend. It took all he had not to ask if she'd asked about him. Mentioned him. Said she wanted him back.

The mug hit the table, jerking him back into the conversation. Both men were staring at him. Had he missed something? "What?"

Lucas's gaze stayed steady. "I asked how you're doing, but you were spaced out."

"Fine. I'm fine."

"You don't look fine. Ever heard of scissors?" Lucas's own hair was close cropped. The server approached. "Trina here might be able to tell you a good place to get a shave." His light brown eyes glinted as he waited for her reaction.

Trina's brown hair was trimmed short. Not quite a buzz cut, but barely long enough to style. It suited her don't-fuck-with-me vibe better than her longer hair had.

Her glare could've melted the stool from under Lucas. It lightened when she looked at him and Caleb. He was only mildly interested in what was going on between the two, and only because he wanted to know if anyone was as miserable as him. "Can I get you two anything?"

"Not going to ask me?" Lucas waggled his mug.

She ignored him. "More of the same?"

Caleb handed her a twenty. "We'll each take one more. Even jackass over here."

Lucas's expression sobered. "Thanks, but I'll pass. I gotta be up early in the morning." His sudden shift made them all give him a second glance, even Trina.

When she left, Caleb scowled at Lucas. "Is this one of those times they talk about the boy being mean because he likes the girl?"

Lucas shook his head. "I can't get a reaction out of her for the life of me. We grew up next to each other."

"Everyone thought you two would end up together. Until you married Shaylee." Caleb shot him a bemused look. "That wedding was legend."

Lucas snorted. "It should've been a sign that the marriage was doomed." He shook his head, his gaze trailing after Trina, who'd disappeared behind the bar. "She won't talk to me unless she's forced to take my order."

A spark of jealousy flared. At least there was still a reason for Lucas to talk to her. But Justin wouldn't cross paths with Priya—ever. They lived on opposite sides of town. All her patients were women. She hardly went to bars. He hardly went out. The only thing binding them together was their friendship.

He missed it. Maybe that's why he was reeling his way past their argument. He missed his friend. How calm she was when Isaiah was bringing down the house around them. Her love of baking. The food she cooked.

Over a month had gone by and at home, he picked up his socks, hung up his towels, and gave Isaiah's toys a regular wash. She'd been right. The shower was easier to clean with that fancy soap. He'd never been a slob, but maybe he'd let things go out of spite. The ultramodern, sanitized life wasn't him, but neither was how he'd lived since returning to Moore.

Earlier today, Justin had wandered through his kitchen, noting the age and inconvenience of everything. The space could use a major upgrade beyond new appliances. The house was forty years old. He could have part of a wall removed and open up the kitchen to the dining room. Make it airy and inviting. Modern. Moore modern. Not upscale-Denver modern.

"Holy shit." Lucas's voice broke through. "Something's going on with you. Who is she?"

Justin's brows dropped. Had Lucas heard something?

It didn't matter, did it? What would happen if people knew he and Priya had slept together? Nothing. She'd go to work. He'd ranch. It wasn't like they were some adored couple that had broken up.

Exclusive friends with benefits. They'd been casual. Because he had no place in his life for a relationship.

Yeah. That was it.

Caleb watched him as he took a swig. When had their new drinks been dropped off? Anyway, the man knew the whole sordid story but he wasn't giving up Justin. And Justin trusted him not to. There weren't many people he trusted. At all.

He never used to be like that, but he'd handed that power over to Gabrielle, too. And Maisy. He'd let their behavior convince him that he couldn't trust anyone. He'd become a borderline hermit.

"Priya Patel." Saying her name was like flipping the

release on a pressure cooker. Caleb sputtered against his bottle. He wasn't the only one surprised that Justin had opened his mouth and told someone about part of his life. "We were sleeping together, trying to keep it casual, and when she wanted more, I…"

"Lost your shit," Lucas supplied as if he'd been there himself.

"Not that bad. Look, do you know what Maisy was like?"

Lucas's gaze strayed to Caleb, like he was seeking permission to answer honestly. Caleb dipped his head and Lucas finally answered. "No offense to the dead, but she was crazy. I don't mean it superficially, but she was a narcissist."

He wasn't expecting Lucas's clarity. The more he was around, the more Justin realized he'd underestimated the guy.

"And the woman I dated before her was exactly the same, only sophisticated about it. White-collar manipulation, and she played me well. It was a very one-sided relationship."

Lucas traced a finger through the condensation of his beer mug. "Relationships where one party holds the power can be toxic."

It sounded like Lucas was better off divorced. But Justin didn't feel better off without Priya. "That's the thing. I felt balanced with Priya. We were friends. Nothing more."

This time Caleb chimed in. "But you were sleeping together."

Then Lucas. "Did you hang out and talk?"

Justin grudgingly answered. "We like the same wine and yeah, I mean, we talked." A lot. "Like I said, we were friends."

"Let me get this straight." Lucas's attention was lost for a second and Justin didn't have to look to know Trina was walking by. "You two hung out, had sex, and played around with your kid together. You probably talked about future plans—just not future plans together—and now that she's gone you feel like your heart's been ripped out, stomped on, and fed to the pigs."

The sympathy in Caleb's gaze unnerved Justin. If he was looking at Justin with pity, there was a reason. "That, my friend, is what you call a relationship."

Misery hung heavy on his shoulders. "I suppose you're going to say 'I told you so.'"

"Nope," Caleb answered. "I do have a few questions though. Are you crazy about her?"

Justin clenched his jaw, afraid to answer.

"Okay. Do you think the risks of a real relationship are worth having her in your life?"

He had to look away. "You said it yourself. She'd make a horrible rancher's wife. She hates my house, wears brand-name clothing, and, honestly, is a tiny bit high-maintenance."

The next words of wisdom came from Lucas. "She's not the rancher. You are. She's a doctor and can buy herself brand-name clothing. I would if I had to look at vaginas all day. I mean, dudes joke about how awesome that would be, but..." He sat back with a shrug. "And all women are a tiny bit high-maintenance."

"Even your sister," Caleb added.

"I don't want to hear about you and Brigit." Though he was slightly curious about how they'd overcome their obstacles. Caleb and Brigit had had a rocky start, but they were a tight couple.

"Brigit organizes the shop," Caleb said. "I dare you to park the riding lawn mower in the wrong spot and leave your tools out after an oil change. I *dare* you."

A hesitant smile lifted his lips. So maybe he was more open to a relationship than he'd thought. "I ruined it. I'm done with the on-again, off-again."

Lucas spread his hands. "But you said you were never on. So ask her to go steady."

Both guys grinned at him like it was the perfect solution.

"I can't just walk up to her door and say, 'Hey, I'm ready to be a thing now.'"

"Nope," Lucas agreed. "You get yourself a haircut, trim the shaggy beard, and find something that doesn't have sheep shit smeared on it. Win her back."

Caleb sat forward. If Justin wasn't careful, these two guys were going to plan the whole affair without him. "Brigit said Priya had some fancy fund-raiser coming up."

"Wait. Brigit talked to Pri?"

"They're friends." Caleb smirked. "Only like, real friends and not—"

"Finish," Justin growled.

"Well, you were a big-shot business guy. Get out your finest suit, knot that tie, and go close the deal."

Close the deal. He'd never been one to back down when his future was riding on the outcome.

CHAPTER 17

The gala fired up all her senses. Natasha had really outdone herself this time.

As Priya lingered in the entrance, she took it all in.

Now she knew how Cinderella felt. The room had cathedral ceilings and a Renaissance style, with swooping chandeliers, and—was that a stained-glass window? Natasha must have connections to have secured this lavish location.

Cream tablecloths and servers wearing crisp white shirts with black vests and bow ties glossed through the room. The lack of a suit coat set them apart from attendees. Men strode around in black tuxes from all the big names. Tom Ford. Stefano Ricci. Burberry.

The evening gowns were dazzling eye candy. She wished she could park a seat in the corner and make the attendees stroll past for her own personal fashion show.

She glanced down to double-check her neckline. Or lack of. The Carolina Herrera gown, borrowed from Natasha, was sleeveless, sleek, and glossy black. A leafy pattern picked out in crystals curved around her bustline and down one side to the top of her thigh. The style was simple and elegant, and the dress was unusually comfortable.

Her shoes were not. The heels had a small platform on the bottom to give her a boost, so she wouldn't have to look up to talk to everyone about challenges in rural health and how bigger children's hospitals like the one her dear friend was raising funds for were critical to her population.

Priya's heart fluttered and nerves fired up her belly. She almost patted her hair, but she dropped her hand and clasped it with her other. She'd have to burn off her adrenaline another way. Given how much she'd paid for the elegant twist secured at the back of her head, she didn't dare touch it.

A familiar face appeared in the crowd. Her stomach clenched, but not in an *ooh, there he is* way. More like *oh, it's him*. Funny how the last six months had made her breakup seem decades old.

Emmett's gaze landed on her and he lifted his chin. The hint of a smile and the sparkle in his dark brown eyes used to turn her insides to goo, but tonight, the mess in her belly was just indigestion.

Only she hadn't eaten, because Natasha was half a size smaller than her. Priya could've afforded a brand-new version of this dress, but she'd rather use a loaner and write a check for Natasha's hospital.

She stiffened. Emmett approached, and since she hadn't left the doorway, she couldn't swoop away and grab an appetizer without it being obvious she was avoiding him. Making him eat his heart out wasn't happening. Happiness wasn't bursting out of her in rainbows and unicorns. She'd been nursing heartbreak for almost a month and a half.

"Pri." Emmett's gaze dropped to her feet and took its time coming back up again. "Gorgeous as always."

She gave the perfunctory smile expected of her. She resented his use of her nickname. But this night wasn't about her. She had no revenge to get. Being with Justin had shown her that she and Emmett were wrong together. When she was with him, she wasn't comfortable enough to be herself. It was when she was with Justin that she'd rediscovered who she really was.

But then, they'd never been together. That was the problem.

Tonight is not about me. And she had to be nice to Emmett. She was here to raise money, and she couldn't risk pissing off Emmett, the star of the night. Rising transplant surgeon on the obsidian edge of technology, with his adept fingers in the latest procedures? He was the one those with deep pockets sought out. Not her.

She gave him her most tolerant smile. "Emmett. Charming as always."

He stopped in front of her, a hand tucked smoothly in his pocket. With the pose he struck, he could be mistaken for a model instead of a talented surgeon. No wonder he was the star of the show. People automatically glanced his way, assessing him, tilting their heads as they planned how to get close to him. Emmett looked like someone you should know.

He thrived on it. And she used to be his, had thrived on being his one and only. He also thrived on being *his* one and only.

"How's birthing babies?" he drawled in a slight Southern accent. It wasn't fake, but he'd worked effortlessly to neutralize his speech. He'd always worried that a kid from Mobile, Alabama, wouldn't be taken seriously as a world-renowned surgeon.

"How's swapping hearts?"

He didn't bother looking at the server as he snagged a champagne flute from a tray. "Good, according to the thirty-five-year-old mother of two that will probably live to see them both graduate."

She bit the inside of her cheek. Take the higher ground. His work was important. So was hers, and she wouldn't demean herself by arguing about it.

A woman who topped her by five inches, wearing a dress that cost at least three grand more than this one originally had, sidled next to Emmett and plucked the glass from his hand. Her dazzling smile brighter than the diamond on her finger. "Are you regaling this poor woman with your stories, dear?"

Emmett chuckled and slipped an arm around her. "She's heard a lot of them. LaShay, this is Priya. She's one of the group I told you about. Pri, this is my fiancée."

LaShay's eyes brightened. "Oh, the group with Natasha?"

It would be easier to be bitter and defensive if the woman didn't seem so nice. As it was, LaShay gushed about Natasha's fund-raising efforts and the quality of the children's hospital. There was no spite in Emmett's date. Only excitement and compassion glittered in her intelligent eyes.

Emmett had not only moved on, but had done so with someone who seemed genuine and was probably skilled and talented in her own right. It's not like Emmett would have settled for less, of course. Priya wanted to feel good about getting over Emmett, even if it was because a sheep rancher had stolen her heart and trashed it. Maybe Emmett would pity her and put her on a bypass machine so she didn't have to deal with the pain of losing someone who didn't love her back.

The night's not about me. If she said that enough, maybe she could get out of the doorway and fund-raise. Then she could tuck herself into bed with a whole bottle of champagne.

"LaShay is a physician, too. A cardiologist." Surprisingly, there was no conceit or pointedness in his tone. Only pride and affection. So *unfair.*

"What's your specialty?" LaShay asked.

"OB/GYN." She hoped LaShay put up with Emmett's superiority complex, or better yet, stabbed him with one of her three-inch stilettos when he got uppity. Since the next question would be where she worked, she answered that as well. "I went back to my hometown in Minnesota to practice."

Emmett's brow furrowed as he frowned. "Wasn't one of the topics of Natasha's seminars about a death at your clinic?"

How had he— A hot flush licked up her spine, flushing her face. The information she'd given Natasha for the case study was supposed to remain anonymous and for educational purposes only as far as patient name and location. But their circle of friends from medical school was close, and Natasha had probably given little thought of mentioning the specifics to him.

Since the confidentiality threshold had been crossed, she had to add a little detail. She didn't have the luxury of being detached from those she treated. "She wasn't just a patient. She was my best friend growing up."

Emmett *tsked*. "Treating friends is tricky. Feelings are bound to get in the way of objectivity."

LaShay's expression morphed into pity, which a touch of well-meaning *you should've known better.*

A deep rumble from behind Priya interjected. "I can't imagine that's possible to avoid in a town of ten thousand." The voice sent spirals of desire through her belly, pooling between her legs. Her body lit up like the chandeliers hanging from the ceiling, sparking to life after too long away from him.

No. She had to be hearing things. But she wasn't.

"Priya treats old classmates, their moms, their grandmas. Another five to ten years, their daughters will be her patients. But a true professional can be objective in spite of their feelings. Or because of, perhaps." Justin ended on a smooth note, a little hint of question with knowing undertones. A guy who could put Emmett in his place, but in a way that would make him agree with everything that was said.

She chanced a look at Justin and did a double take. Gone was the scruffy beard. Cleanly shaven, his hard jaw was prominent and—was that a cleft in his chin? He'd trimmed his hair, too. Tapered, the longer hair on the top was smartly combed to the side. His keen gaze was planted directly on her.

"Justin. What are you—"

"Sorry I'm late." Justin grinned at Emmett and LaShay. That calculating smile. This was the man who closed deals in the boardroom. She'd stupidly assumed that room was more like the small staff lounge in the hospital.

But, no. This guy was comfortable in his Tom Ford tux, the one she'd gushed over.

He leaned toward Emmett like he was telling them a secret. "I didn't think I could come, and I had to do some of the toughest negotiations in my career with Natasha to score an invite."

Priya feathered her fingers across her collarbone. Damn her nerves. "And how did you score an invite?"

That grin was aimed in her direction. She almost sighed, but the effect was too powerful. "Other than begging to be your plus-one? I spent plenty of years making stupid money before I settled into sheep ranching. Now I can put some of it to good use." He cocked his head. "If you can convince me."

LaShay's tinkling laughter cut between them. "A sheep rancher with deep pockets. Sounds absolutely juicy. We'll have to plan a meet up before the weekend is over." She glanced over her shoulder at the ballroom floor. "But speaking of raising money, we'd better go work the crowd."

She dragged Emmett away, but Emmett cast one last

furtive glance between her and Justin. What was her ex's perplexed expression for? He didn't believe she could've, or would've, moved on after him? Or was her own expression so full of disbelief and indecision that he was concerned?

No time for Emmett. Justin was here.

"What are you doing here?" she asked tightly.

"Apologizing."

She stared at him. Where was that server with all the champagne?

"You look beautiful," he whispered, his voice full of longing.

"You'll have to do better. I was already called gorgeous tonight."

He shoved his hands in his pockets. Were those suits designed just to make the male figure more devastating? It didn't help that she knew what he looked like underneath it. "By who? The ex with the fiancée with the giant rock?"

"Yes. That's Emmett. The one I never told you about," she said flatly.

He winced. "Priya."

"Save it. I'm here to raise money for a worthy cause and I've been standing around long enough." She spun on a heel and promptly lost her balance.

Justin caught her elbow and steadied her. "When this shindig is done, we're talking. *Really* talking."

She pinned him with a hard glare.

He softened his grip, then reluctantly released her. "Hear me out. Please."

"Only if you think you can do the same." Switching her concentration back to staying upright, she strutted away.

∽

THAT ASS. He drank in the sight of her rounded backside swaying away like a man who'd been stranded in a desert for a week. She was upset with him, and he couldn't blame her. She'd put herself out there and he'd scorned her. He was willing to do his penance and win her back.

His check was already written, his donation made to the children's hospital. Tonight, his only mission was winning Priya Patel back. But first, he'd wait for her to work the crowd like Natasha had warned him she needed to. Priya was here for a more important reason than both of them.

I'll let you come if you can be her most fabulous arm candy. Her ex just told me that he recently got engaged and his fiancée will be there. I haven't had a free moment to tell her. Oh, and how much can you donate?

His mouth quirked. That conversation had been a ride. Her ex was a distinguished man who exuded confidence and intelligence. Money. Style. Taste. He saved lives and still had time for eighteen holes at the country club. Priya could have a guy like that. But instead, she'd wanted to be with a sheep rancher.

What the hell had he been thinking? That *she* would coerce him into a relationship? He'd realized way too fucking late he should be thanking every star in the sky that he was the one she'd chosen to be with.

He scanned the elegant ballroom. This wasn't his first black-tie event, but at the moment, it felt like the most critical, despite the fact he didn't have a dime riding on the outcome. Only his heart.

The next two hours, he worked the room. Anyone who wasn't already engaged in conversation, he hit up.

Are you a doctor or a donor? I'm here with an OB/GYN. She delivered my son. Saved him, actually. Our little town has less than ten thousand people, and his mom was taken by a sudden illness. If Dr. Patel hadn't operated when she had, he would've had severe complications. Where we're at, the ambulance ride to a bigger hospital would take at least an hour. And getting a life-flight plane or helicopter wouldn't have saved my son. This was summer. In winter, the weather can put a stop to anything with an engine. Then he went to his speech about how Natasha's children's hospitals helped provide long-distance support and care until children could get to a bigger facility.

It wasn't long before he'd gathered groups of people to listen to the story of Isaiah's birth. One he'd gladly tell over and over if it would benefit more kids.

Once the latest crowd dispersed to talk finances and arrange donations, a waiter skirted around him, pausing long enough for Justin to grab a drink. He refrained from draining the flute like a shot glass. He wasn't used to all this talking.

Priya appeared at his shoulder, a bemused expression across her pretty face. She stopped next to him, shoulder to shoulder. He turned to face her. She hardly wore any makeup. Her thick, dark lashes framed her golden eyes better than any mascara could. A touch of glittery shadow was powdered across her lids, and any gloss or lipstick she had donned was long gone. He liked her natural lip color better.

She glanced sideways at him. "I think you've scored yourself an invite to every fund-raiser Natasha puts on."

"They like hearing my perspective."

"You make them like hearing it. A handsome single father gushing about how well his baby came out of a traumatic situation." She rolled her eyes toward him. "You make me sound like a hero."

She still wasn't facing him, so he stepped in front of her. "Two things. One, you are a hero. You're not just my hero, but you're the hero of every baby and mom you treat. You're the hero of every nineteen-year-old whose ovarian cancer symptoms were blown off by her regular doctor. You're the champion of every woman trying to talk herself out of a—what do you ladies call them? Slammogram?"

The corner of her mouth lifted. "It's my duty as a doctor."

"And it's Caleb's duty to pull people out of burning buildings and car wrecks. He even gets paid for it. Yet we still call firemen our heroes. You, Priya Patel, don't get to decide."

"All right. What's the second thing?"

He let a slow smile spread across his face. "You think I'm handsome?"

She huffed but couldn't hold back a laugh. "That's what you gleaned from my comment?"

He rubbed his bare face. Clean-shaven wasn't bad, but the beard had grown on him. "It's the new look, right? And my haircut?"

"It's the expensive suit that looks like it was sewn onto your body."

"This old thang?"

She chuckled, but her smile faded. "Why are you here, Justin?"

"To prove how sorry I am." If only she'd tell him what he needed to do to make it right between them, to reignite the magic that still simmered, ready to boil. The only ingredient missing was her trust. Her trust that he wouldn't hurt her, and that he'd always support her.

"Why? You were right. We were supposed to be friends and we didn't open up to each other." She paused to chew her lower lip, something he missed doing so badly. "And you were also right that I lied. Once you and I grew close, I should've told you what Maisy said. I should've trusted you enough to confide in you about that."

"I thought a lot about that, and what you said about hiding behind the actions of the women in my past. Maisy put you in a tough situation. She used your job as a way to confess what she'd done without facing any consequences, hurting both of us." It had taken him too long to see it.

"I've been talking to Katherine and Martin."

He smiled. Katherine had been so relieved when she'd last spoken of Priya. "I heard. They adore you. Two of your biggest supporters, and everyone with a vagina Katherine runs across is going to get glowing recommendations about you. She singlehandedly dismantled any rumor mill regarding you and quality care."

"I missed them." A gentle crease formed in her brow and her eyes misted over. "Between us, we actually have a lot of decent memories under the hurt."

"I'd like to think we're like that."

"Oh, Justin." She sniffled. "I wanted more, and you didn't. I've learned to be okay with it."

"I'm not. I didn't know what I wanted." He wished he could make himself sound like a deal she couldn't refuse. "Actually, I had what I wanted, and I was too scared to realize it. I took it out on you. I took everything out on you. You got me through the toughest time of my life. Not only did you get me through, you made me look forward to each day. I knew that as long as you were around, I would be okay, and my son would be okay."

Her eyes glistened with moisture. "How is he?"

She missed Isaiah. How could he have been so oblivious? She'd rocked him to sleep. Fed him. Rejoiced when he hit all his milestones. Isaiah wasn't just *his* kid. He was important to her. And she hadn't gotten to see him for six weeks.

"I'm sorry. I didn't realize that not seeing him..." He pinched the bridge of his nose. *Do better, Justin.* Complete honesty between them. "She didn't just use me. Gabrielle. She convinced me to change myself. I went from the kid you knew in high school to this guy." Waving a hand down his body, he scowled. "I was avoiding my family because each time I came home, it reminded me that I'd always wanted to come home. I like Wrangler's and Levi's jeans. I prefer boots to loafers. Farming and ranching is in my blood and I don't want to sanitize it."

"And you thought I was doing that with my soap in the shower?" He couldn't fault the blush of sarcasm in her voice. She'd been nothing like Gabrielle. Or Maisy.

"I was afraid because you could've. I would figure out any way possible to make you happy. As long as I get to sit by your side every night, clinking our glasses of wine together and talking about everything under the big blue sky."

She blinked back the moisture in her eyes. "I think I proved I wasn't farm wife material."

"Because you're a doctor. I'm not asking you to deliver lambs and treat hoof rot and help me with shots. I have business partners that I happen to be related to. I'm looking for a woman to spend my life with." Not just any woman. Her.

"That's a bold statement coming from you."

"It's the truth. And I'll let you in on a little secret."

She tilted her head. He had her hooked, but how would she react?

"It turns out, we were actually in a relationship."

She didn't lose her apprehension. "Yes. We even had a name for it."

The benefits thing. She was so much more than a friend. "You had the courage to tell me when you wanted more, and I chickened out."

"I chickened out, too." She clutched her hands together. "I was jealous of Devya because she got all the attention. I'm almost thirty damn years old and I was as envious as a ten-year-old. And Mom and Dad? Gallivanting around the globe? I should've been happy for them, but I felt abandoned. They don't tell you that you can feel like that as an adult." She made a disgusted noise. "I felt sorry for myself and I was too ashamed to admit that to you."

He knew her parents' inattention had bothered her. "You'd been away for years, but when you came home, they kept living like you were gone."

"Right? For good reason. They *should* travel while they're still healthy enough to." She rushed on, like he'd opened the gates to greener pastures. "I had no friends. They didn't know that. *I* didn't even realize that. I hid behind Maisy as much as she hid behind me. My job? I was losing all my patients, wondering what was wrong with me, but you were raising a son all by yourself and running a business. It seemed…insignificant."

He drifted close enough to put his hands on her shoulders. "And Emmett made you feel insignificant, so you didn't talk about him either. I understand that. I failed when I kept my walls up. I didn't let you know how important you are to me. How important you are to my son. And how I want to know everything about you. I'm in love with you, Priya."

Her eyes widened, the whites practically glowing. The way the lights danced in her irises only highlighted how stunning she was. "You can't…" She shook her head. That's right. She knew very well he wouldn't say anything he didn't mean. "Why now? What in the last month made you think that suddenly you're not only ready for a real relationship, but for one with me?"

"Not having you around was a pretty good wake-up call. And how you didn't try to contact me. You moved on."

"I missed you," she whispered.

It was hearing that she'd missed him, but seeing that she was moving on without him, that broke the remnants of any walls remaining. He had one last fear of hers to lay to rest.

"Katherine and Martin mentioned seeing you. Then they said that I don't talk about you as much as I used to. 'Used to ramble on and on' were the words they used. Katherine asked if we had been seeing each other quietly because of everything and if that everything broke us up. I said I screwed up and would do anything to get you back."

Her gaze sharpened and fear simmered in her golden depths. "How did they take it?"

"They're watching Isaiah so I can be here."

Her eyes glistened, and she pressed her lips together.

He stroked the back of his finger down her cheek. "I didn't mean to make you cry."

"I've cried a lot over you."

Instead of dropping his hand at the shame running through him, he moved even closer until they were barely touching. "I'm so sorry I hurt you."

She blinked and looked up at him. "It wouldn't have been so hard if I didn't love you, too."

"Can we love each other together?" He pressed a soft kiss on the corner of her mouth. "Can we talk all night over a glass of wine when we're not tangled together in my freshly washed sheets? Can you go and do all your doctoring while I go and do all my ranching and we'll tell each other all about it afterward?" He planted another light kiss on the other side of her mouth. "Will you complete my little family?"

"You have a huge family." She smiled as she said it. "And the best baby in the world." When she slipped her arms around his shoulders, he wanted to rejoice. "Do you want more kids?"

"Only if you do. And whenever you do. And only if you stick around to help me." He grinned. "But what are the odds that two babies in a row can have colic?" The look she gave him stopped his laughter. "Then you gotta promise to stick around. We make a good team."

"One more thing. I'm going to Paris this summer to see

my sister. You're welcome to come, and if you can't, I'm going anyway."

"We'll recruit some grandparents and have a getaway."

She brushed her hands along his shoulders and gave his biceps an appreciative squeeze. "If you want to grow that beard back, I won't complain."

"So will you do it?" Priya arranged shirts, capris, and skirts in the suitcase. The clothing was folded and rolled, then lined up next to each other. She fiddled with the spacing, going for maximum space optimization now that she had more than her belongings to pack.

Justin spun around. Isaiah was swaddled against his body with a baby wrap. "You're looking at the newest baby-wearing model."

Priya straightened from her task and grinned. Krista had asked if Justin could help her out with the baby-wearing workshops. She had plenty of mom models. "Men everywhere will jump on the trend."

"They already are, I'm telling you. We're not a secret society." He scanned the clothing arranged in organized piles on the bed. "Packing already?"

Their flight to Paris didn't leave for five days. "I thought since I not only have to pack for me, but you, too, and we have to get Isaiah ready—"

Justin took two large steps toward her, turned so he didn't crush Isaiah between them, and tucked her in tight for kiss. The brush of his whiskers tickled her chin. She loved the feel. He kept it trimmed short, and when he had his cowboy hat on, she could barely keep her hands to herself until Isaiah was in bed for the night.

Of course, they didn't always wait. They'd mastered the quickie.

When he broke contact, he murmured, "I told you, your organization is sexy. Pack as early as you want."

She didn't have to pack for Isaiah. Justin's parents were coming for the week, but she wanted all his stuff washed and ready.

Justin went to the closet and took out his suit. "Think we'll need this?"

She cocked a brow. "You hate wearing that."

"I love how you take it off."

"Then pack it." She might need to borrow another dress. Recreating the night they'd made up at the fund-raiser was another fantasy she hadn't known she had.

He dropped the tux next to the pile she'd gathered.

"Hey, did I tell you they hired a new OB?" She would've— they talked every night she wasn't called to the hospital—but the new hire had been announced at the end of her shift. "She heard about Moore through Natasha's fund-raiser and the workshops she gave. But I think it was your sales pitch that really sold the clinic."

"Do we have our invites for next year yet?" He grinned, knowing full well Natasha had begged her to bring him back each year.

She returned the smile as a savory scent teased her nose. "Is that…"

"Vegetarian chili and pav buns. Your nana sent me the recipe."

Her grandparents were so excited to see them. Grandma and Grandpa Saunders had been out for a grill party Justin had thrown earlier, along with his siblings and her parents. Between Justin and Isaiah, work buddies, and taking advantage of Isaiah's sleepover with the Jorgensons, her social calendar was packed—along with her work schedule. Word of mouth, thanks to vocal new patients like Brigit—due in December.

Life was good. She'd told him once that it was okay if he didn't give up on someone. She was grateful he hadn't given up on them.

JUSTIN BOUNCED LIGHTLY. Both he and Isaiah watched Priya rush from the room as soon as the dryer buzzed. Normally, he'd offer to grab the load so she could keep packing, but he had his own item to pack.

Once she was elbow-deep in warm baby clothes, he retrieved a little rounded velvet box from the top of the closet. Yes, he'd used his height advantage over Priya to hide his gift.

Swiftly, he refolded the box inside of a pair of his socks and wedged it back into the suitcase. Even if she rearranged their belongings, she shouldn't pick up on the hidden jewelry box. He'd gotten the smallest he could for maximum hiding capability.

His proposal was all planned out. He'd even called Devya to help make the night happen, and his ear was still ringing from her screech.

The engagement ring he'd bought was part of a matching set. And he'd had both bands engraved.

The inside of her delicate band was inscribed with *Rancher's Wife*.

And on the inside of his was *Doctor's Husband*.

. . .

Lucas and Trina have some hurdles to get over in Rancher Next Door. They've each been hurt in the past and it's affecting their ability to accept love in the present.

I'd love to hear what you thought. You can drop a quick review of White Collar Rancher the retailer.

For all the latest news, sneak peeks, quarterly short stories, and free material sign up for my newsletter.

ABOUT THE AUTHOR

Marie Johnston writes paranormal and contemporary romance and has collected several awards in both genres. Before she was a writer, she was a microbiologist. Depending on the situation, she can be oddly unconcerned about germs or weirdly phobic. She's also a licensed medical technician and has worked as a public health microbiologist and as a lab tech in hospital and clinic labs. Marie's been a volunteer EMT, a college instructor, a security guard, a phlebotomist, a hotel clerk, and a coffee pourer in a bingo hall. All fodder for a writer!! She's married with four kids.

mariejohnstonwriter.com
Facebook
Twitter @mjohnstonwriter
Instagram @mariejohnstonwriter

ALSO BY MARIE JOHNSTON

Part-Time Cowboys
Rancher in Training (Book 1)
Red Hot Rancher (Book 2)
White Collar Rancher (Book 3)
Rancher Next Door (Book 4)
Her Christmas Offer (novella)

www.ingramcontent.com/pod-product-compliance
Lightning Source LLC
Chambersburg PA
CBHW050400190726
48284CB00007BB/2372